Monochrome Sunset

+ Seven Short Stories

Alastair M. Hart

Cover design by Scott Gaunt: scottgaunt@hotmail.co.uk

ISBN: 9798474484754

PublishNation
www.publishnation.co.uk

Dedicated to:-

To SIFA-RESEARCH
(Suicide Intervention First Aid)
www.sifa-research.org

A donation from the Kindle and Paperback versions of this book will go to SIFA-Research.

Contents

Monochrome Sunset

Music pulsed through the stadium, like a tidal wave rippling over the people who were enraptured by a man they saw as a god. Thousands of voices screamed in adulation, their furious worship almost drowning out the music itself. He stood there, the spotlight beaming on him, illuminating him as though he was a fallen angel. Anguish was etched upon his face as he sang his heart out, tearing emotions out of his soul the same way he did night after night, giving the audience so many intimate parts of himself that I didn't know how much of himself he had left. How much could one man give before he had given it all?

The electric guitar thrummed and the bass rumbled. The drums crashed, but they were all secondary to his wonderful, angelic voice, and the words he created. I stood to the side of the stage, watching in awe at what I can only describe as magic. The way Drew sang was as though he was conjuring spells, enchanting and bewitching those who listened, a modern day Pied Piper who coaxed millions upon millions of fans to listen to him. To look at him up there was to see a god touching his followers. The sheer passion that emanated from the crowd was evangelical and, if I'm honest, it did scare me a little.

Drew ended the song and the last word hung in the air, as beautiful as the sensual moon. He let his head drop and he raised his fist, punching the air. The crowd followed suit, but where he was silent they all cheered and hollered and whooped. They stamped their feet and I was afraid that the entire world was going to crack like an egg. The intensity of their emotion was terrifying and I couldn't imagine how Drew felt about it. But I was struck by something profound as I gazed at him from the edge of the stage, something that perhaps only I noticed.

For all the adulation he was receiving and all the millions of fans, he looked alone and vulnerable. He looked tired. He raised his other arm and his head, tilting his neck back as the wave of love and appreciation came to him, echoing what he had given them. The music faded into silence as the lights went down and darkness swallowed him. But while the music stopped, the cheering didn't. The crowd cried out for more, demanding that he do their bidding.

It struck me then that people could be ever so demanding of their gods.

When he staggered away from the stage and returned to his dressing room, he looked haggard and drained. His shoulders were slumped and there were shadows under his eyes. He leaned against the wall for support and then disappeared into his sanctuary where he could be away from the world for a little while, where he could shower and cleanse his body, where he could peel the sweat soaked clothes off his skin. I watched with a mixture of awe and pity. I remembered a time long ago, a simpler time when we were just two kids messing about in his basement.

*

"Okay, Jamie, let's try a little bit of this," Drew said. He counted down with his fingers and then, as soon as he launched into the song, I knew that something special was happening. He closed his eyes and the voice that poured out of his mouth wasn't anything that I had expected. My skin tingled and, after a few moments, I realized that I was holding my breath. Drew sang a song that was not his own. In fact, it was a popular song that had been covered by a range of different artists and yet, when he sang, the song seemed fresh and reborn. He was making it his own. Even then I knew he had a unique ability to imbue his words with emotions and somehow make the song transcend the trappings of its lyrics. He was a singer in the very best sense of the term, an artist, bringing the song to life, fusing emotion with melody in one glorious canvas.

When he stopped singing, he averted his gaze and looked bashful.

I clapped.

"Drew, that was amazing! Where the hell did that come from? How long have you been able to sing like that?"

Drew shrugged. "I don't know. Always have done, I guess, just haven't been comfortable with people listening."

"Well, people should listen. We need to get your voice out there. This could be huge!"

"I don't know about that," he shot me a slanting glance and clasped his hands in his lap, looking down at them. "I don't think anyone else would want to hear me sing."

"Are you crazy? Drew, did you not just hear yourself?" Drew looked at me blankly. I pulled out my phone and asked him to sing again, this time recording it. When I played it back, he still seemed nonplussed about what he was hearing and I thought it a shame that someone with such a talent could not even realize it. When I look back on it now, I realize that it wasn't that he wasn't aware of his talent; it was that he was afraid of me. Even though we were friends, at the time he couldn't bring himself to tell me that, but that's Drew all over. He's never been good at sharing his feelings, at least not with anyone who is close to him.

"Sing something else!" I urged. He did and I recorded it, and we spent almost the whole night trying out various different songs. There wasn't anything that couldn't be transformed into *his* song. I had never heard anything like it before and I wondered if this was what Sam Phillips had felt like the first time he had heard Elvis sing. It was just so...so *magical*. Sometimes in life you get a feeling about things, a feeling that one moment can change your entire life. Usually it's when you fall in love or when you hold your child for the first time, but for me it was when I sat there listening to Drew. I just knew that we could have something special.

"Drew, how about tomorrow I bring some recording equipment over and we do this properly? You deserve to be heard. A voice like yours shouldn't be hidden away from the world."

"I don't know, do you really think people will want to listen to me?"

"Drew, I promise you, this is going to be big. *You* are going to be big. I've listened to a hell of a lot of music and I haven't ever heard anything like you. We need to get this out there."

My mind was swimming with possibilities. I knew that he could be as big as Elvis or The Beatles. My heart thumped and I couldn't sleep. I dreamed of bright lights and huge crowds, of people cheering his name, and I wanted to be along for the ride. Even though I had always loved music, I'd never been a top tier talent. I could carry a tune and I could hold the rhythm of a song with a few instruments, but I lacked that innate kernel of talent that separated the best from the rest of us. But that didn't matter. I could recognize talent when I saw it and I knew that I would do anything I could to help Drew reach his potential and shake this world up.

It was a simpler time. We were just teenagers and we couldn't comprehend the true complexity and nuance of the world. It felt as though one song could change the world and nothing could be better than that.

*

After I helped pack up the sound equipment after the concert, I went to Drew's dressing room. There were still a few roadies hauling the heavier equipment off the stage. The crowd had dissipated, although there were a few stragglers still high on the rolling music and probably high on a few other things as well. They swayed to music that was still echoing through their minds, while the rest of them were home now, reflecting on being in the presence of greatness. Now that the bright lights of the stage had been turned off, I could see the stars in all their glory. They twinkled brightly overhead and the moon was full and sensual, swelling with ethereal beauty. As I stood on the stage, I looked out at the vast, empty arena, which was bathed in shadow. I reached out with my hand, as though I was trying to summon even just a shadow of the emotion that Drew must have felt, but there was nothing there. I would never be as loved as he was. So many strangers, all devoted to him. I would never know what that felt like.

When I returned inside, I was met with the sounds of the roadies and other staff chatting and joking around, relaxing with some beers. I nodded to them as I passed and then disappeared into Drew's dressing room. He was out of the shower. A towel wrapped around his waist and covered the lower half of his body. The top half glistened with water that hadn't dried. His long hair looked darker as it caressed his rounded shoulders. He looked down at the floor, holding a bottle of water in his hands. A tattoo of a snake slithered across the top of his back and other illustrations and notes were peppered over his pale skin. A TV played in the background, scrolling through news. Neither of us paid attention to it.

"Great show tonight, Drew," I said.

Drew grunted. He ran a hand through his hair, pushing it back, revealing his tired eyes. "Aren't they all?" he sighed.

"Can you believe it's only been five years?" I walked to a nearby table and picked up a few snacks that had been laid out for him.

"Feels like a lifetime," Drew said. After a few moments later, he continued. "I mean it, Jamie. I feel so tired, like I've given so much and I don't have anything else to give. I don't know how much longer I can go on. I feel old before my time."

"You could have fooled me. You were up on that stage running around like the Tasmanian Devil. Just rest up for the night. I'm sure you'll be fine."

"No, I won't be. There's something in here," he prodded the middle of his chest. "I love being out on that stage, but then something happens and I just...I just can't seem to be at peace. I know that everything else is going to come at me and I'm tired of it. Why can't it just be about the music?"

"That's not the way the world works. Things are more complicated than that. You're larger than life, Drew. A part of you belongs to them now."

Drew wore a sardonic smile. "I know, but a part of me isn't enough, is it? They won't stop until they have all of me. I'm just a puppet to them. They want to tear me down and strip me of my flesh, taking a piece of me for themselves, as though that would make their lives any better."

"You're just tired. It'll be okay," I said, worried for my friend. There were moments when he sank into gloom and despair, and seemed for all the world to be lost. I tried to imagine what it was like to be him, to have all those people vying for his attention, envious of his majesty. Despite being a witness to his journey over the past five years, there were things that I could never understand. Despite how close we were, there were parts of him that I could never see.

"No, it won't. I already know what it's going to be like. They're going to tear me apart again. They're going to want to do features and spreads and try and get me to sing their songs. They're going to swarm around my house as though I'm some kind of saviour. I've not been sent from heaven. I don't know why they think I'm going to make a difference in their lives. I'm just a singer. Why can't they let me sing?"

"People are always looking for ways to make their lives better. Sometimes they can't find it in themselves, so they look to other people. You touch their hearts, Drew. You make them feel something that they can't get themselves. Hearing you sing is like looking out into the infinity of space. It makes them feel connected to the world in a profound. It just so happens that you're the conduit for that."

"But I never asked for this," Drew said in a small voice.

It was true – he hadn't – but there were plenty of people who did and plenty of people who would have given anything to be in his position. But not all of them had seen the toll it had taken on him. They only saw the fame and the glory. They didn't realize how much it took from him. Guilt swelled in my heart for the part I had played in his rise to fame. If it hadn't been for me pushing him, he might never have shared his gift with the world and he might never have had things ripped away from him. I knew that I was responsible for this and I had to make it right. I had been working on an idea, chasing a rumour I had heard being whispered among the world of celebrities, but I hadn't suggested it to Drew yet. I didn't know if he would go for it or not, but if he was done with this world, then perhaps he was ready to move on to the next.

*

Drew and I had been working on his sound for a while now. We managed to book a gig at one of his Dad's friend's parties. It was for a fortieth birthday, I think, although I don't remember the details. Usually a DJ would have played this party, going through all the hits, punching through the silence with nostalgia to remind everyone of a better time when they were younger and the world seemed filled with opportunities. At that moment, I wondered when I would reach that point, when would I start to look back instead of forward and wonder what might have been? It turned out that it would be sooner than I could ever realize, although I didn't know it that at the time.

Drew was immensely nervous before he took to the stage. It was one thing singing in our rooms and quite another to face a crowd. He was trembling so fiercely and looked so pale that I worried he might pass out. There was only so much I could do from backstage. Although I was on this journey with him, there were parts he had to walk alone and I could only stand by and watch and pray that he would be able to endure everything he needed to endure.

As he took to the stage, people looked up at him in silent expectation, wondering what this young boy could do that a DJ couldn't. A few of them, fuelled by alcohol, yelled encouragement. Drew looked across at me and I gave him an approving nod. He closed his eyes and clutched the microphone as tightly as a drowning man would cling to a life raft. Then, he began to sing and I saw it on their faces. I saw the look that must have been on my face the first time I had heard him. They were transported to another world, a world where beautiful things lived. After just one song, he had them in the palm of his hand. Drew grew in confidence, feeding off the aura of the crowd, getting braver in his gestures. He strode across the stage, using all the space to his benefit, and his voice filled the room. The crowd sang along with him. They laughed and cheered and, when he was finished, they applauded until their hands were sore.

Drew stumbled off the stage with a huge grin on his face, looking delirious. Back then, it was still all new to him.

"I think they want one more," I nodded towards the stage. The crowd were chanting for Drew to come back, so he obliged. He ended up doing more than one more; it was the first sign of how much people were going to demand of him. He looked dazed when he came off for the final time. I thought that he might sing for the rest of the night.

And then, as we were standing beside the stage, talking about our plans for the future, a girl approached. Her name was Marie and she was the most beautiful girl I had ever seen, but, of course, I was just a mannequin to her. Drew was the one she wanted to talk to. She gave me a polite smile, but when she looked at Drew, her entire face lit up as though it was illuminated by the Aurora Borealis. There was a spark to her that was infectious and it was clear that she had already fallen in love with him, even if she was yet unaware of it. I wasn't sure if Drew had noticed, but he seemed to enjoy the attention.

I slipped away, leaving them to their privacy. Up until that moment, Drew had always had difficulty speaking with girls, but here was a perfect girl approaching him. That was just one of the many benefits of fame, but it also came with a price.

Over the years, some people have assumed that I was jealous upon Marie's arrival – after all, there have always been horror stories about women breaking up successful partnerships – but the fact is I welcomed her into our lives. She helped Drew centre himself in a way that I never could. She got him to open up about his emotions in a way that I had never been able to and he seemed all the better for it. She was an avid supporter of Drew and was always ready to make a cup of tea or bring us some snacks. She even offered alternative perspectives on the songs Drew sang and how we put them together. The duo had transformed into a trio and, when I looked at them, I had the sense that the two of them were going to be together forever. Sometimes you just get the feeling that things are meant to be and that's what I felt when I looked at them.

I should have known that things were never going to be that simple.

Even though I wasn't resentful of her specifically, I was envious of what they shared. I hoped to find companionship like that myself someday. Now though, after how it ended, maybe it's better that I didn't. The most intense emotions are the ones that can scorch you; perhaps it's better that I've remained immune to these things.

But still, it's always sad to think of those times and how brightly the sun shone knowing how it all ended. I can still hear the laughter we shared echoing through the halls of destiny. In that moment, the three of us had the world at our feet and we felt invincible.

*

"This is about her, isn't it?" I asked. Water dripped from Drew's body onto the floor. His feet were bare and I couldn't understand how he wasn't freezing. There was probably still a lot of adrenaline rushing through his system. It always took him some time to calm down after a gig. He sipped his water, which was a good sign.

"Isn't it always about her?" he asked.

"Come on, Drew... I know it's hard, but at some point you're going to have to let her go," I tried to speak as gently as I possibly could, even though I knew the words were harsh. The sunken pits that were his eyes glared at me. He wiped an errant tear away from one of them.

"You know I can't ever do that," he said.

I sighed and let the silence settle over us. I could feel the void that filled the room, one that could only have been made bearable by her. But the price of this life was high.

"You know," Drew continued, "I never felt like I gave her everything I could. There was always more. There was always something I was holding back. I give it all to them," he gestured lazily with one hand towards the vague direction of the stage, "but I couldn't give it all to her. Maybe that's why she's gone."

"You know that's not the reason why. You can't blame yourself."

"Can't I?" he looked up, his eyes wild, black strands of hair matted against his forehead. "Why else did this happen? If it hadn't been for me and my fame, then she would still be by my side. If I hadn't been so famous, then we'd be living in a nice little house somewhere, perhaps with a family. I think I'd quite like a child. I've always liked the idea of raising a family, teaching the children all about the world and how to make it a better place."

"You still could..." I said in a faltering voice. He glared at me.

"You know I can't. Why would I want to bring a child into this? And I couldn't anyway, not without her. It wouldn't be fair. I can barely handle it myself. What kind of life would my child have? It's bad enough that a whole lot of me belongs to the world. If I had a kid, they'd take them and make them theirs. I don't know if I could bear that. Maybe I'm being selfish, but if I have a kid, I'd want them to be mine and mine alone, at least when they're younger. And they wouldn't be able to have an upbringing like we did. They wouldn't learn about the world; they'd just have everything handed to them. And they'd have everyone interested in their business. I couldn't handle a kid being raised with the eyes of the world on them. What kind of life would it be for them? They'd be in a zoo. It's bad enough for me, but for a kid? No... I couldn't condemn them like that. Anyway, it wouldn't be right to have a kid without Marie. We always talked about it, you know? We used to lie in bed at night and think about what our child would be like. Marie would joke that she'd get the worst of both worlds, that she would end up looking like me and sounding like her." His lips twitched into a smile and, for a moment, the gloom receded from his face. For a moment, he looked happy again, but, as the memory faded, so did his mood.

"You could always try again. There are other women out there," I said half-heartedly, knowing what he would say.

"There's only one Marie. And I can't get her back. She was my future, but now she's only my past. I don't have a future without her." He choked on the last words and his head hung once again. The bottle of water he had been holding dropped to the floor as he held his head in his hands, his fingers looking like pale trees covered in obsidian leaves. I closed my eyes and hung my head as well, wishing that things hadn't ended with Marie as they had done.

*

The rise had been meteoric. Drew's music had captured the hearts and minds of so many people. Videos of his went viral online, drawing in a huge following, as though he had burst on the scene from nowhere. Marie and I were fielding calls from all sorts of people asking about his background and if he had had any official training. We recorded so much in those days. His ever-growing fan base wanted more and more, so we gave it to them. It was no good drip feeding them anything. They were ravenous and rabid, and if we stopped giving them songs they would have moved on to something else.

But Drew managed to capture their attention. Every song he sang sounded fresh, even the tired old classics that he had played. Messages hurled in over cyberspace, declaring love for him. There were some trolls, of course, vicious messages that had no place in polite society, but they were drowned by the positive comments. We could record tracks and videos from our basements and post them online. We even streamed live concerts so that people could feel as though they were a part of something. We started to create merchandise and, for a time, it seemed like an adventure, but there was always a feeling that it would come to an end. There was always the sense that eventually people would get bored and move on. At least that's how Drew felt. Marie and I were a little more confident in his abilities.

Soon enough, official offers started pouring in from record companies that saw his potential and wanted to make a star out of him. We fielded all the offers and discussed them as a group, as we always did, and then took the one we thought would fit Drew the best. His first album broke all kinds of records and he continued with the virtual concerts so that people from all over the world could experience what he had to offer. Of course, seeing it online was nothing compared to the grandeur of seeing him in person. I felt privileged to be close to him on a daily basis, to see him twist words like spells in the air.

Something magical happened during his first live concert. People stood before him like devout worshippers and I could see the moment in which they were enraptured by him. Their eyes lit up with love and devotion, and I wondered if he could sense the importance of this moment. From then on, his life would never be the same. They would always be there to defend and deride him. His fans could be the sturdiest shield ,as well as the sharpest sword, as he would find out eventually.

As his fame grew, people became more aware of his personal life and the people in it. Of course, there were a lot of fans who convinced themselves that he loved them and that the words he sang were meant for them and only them, despite them reaching millions of pairs of ears. They were fanatic in their devotion and Drew was sent all manner of things. There were love notes, phone numbers, locks of hair and even underwear. Marie didn't appreciate this at all and she tried to get Drew to send a message out, but none of his fans listened. Marie bore the brunt of their jealousy. She was seen as some kind of temptress, trapping Drew from experiencing true love with them. But they only knew the Drew they had built in their mind, not the man himself, not the man that had given his heart and soul to Marie. What they didn't understand, what they could never understand, was that every song Drew sang was for Marie, not for them.

But they were convinced that he belonged to them.

In hindsight, I suppose there were things we could have done differently, but we never expected what would happen next. As time wore on and Drew's fame exploded, the attention he got weighed on him so much that everything was beginning to buckle. I could see cracks beginning to form between him and Marie. All the beautiful girls that were sending him lascivious messages and nude photos, all the rumours fuelled by tabloid papers and gossip rags started to plant seeds of doubt. I think there was a part of Marie, a part she hated, that saw Drew cheating on her as inevitable. After all, what man could resist temptation for so long? It was like flinging candy at a child. Eventually, the child was going to gorge itself. Marie started to become withdrawn and Drew tried his best to make her realize that she was the only one for him. I couldn't fault his efforts, but it always felt as though he was fighting a losing battle. I tried to convince her as well, but the doubts had taken full hold in her mind and she became erratic. She used to shut herself in her room and be consumed with reading all the rumours and comments about her. People were nasty. They didn't think Marie deserved Drew.

They couldn't be alone. They couldn't be a couple because they had millions of chattering voices nagging and gnawing at them. There was only so much they could take. Drew was being pulled apart. He loved singing and didn't want to do anything else, but the toll it was taking on his relationship was too much to bear. There seemed to only be one end. Drew wanted a family. He wanted Marie. He loved her more than he loved music; it was as simple as that. In a way, he loved her more than he loved life itself. He was unable to change the minds of his fans, so when the time came to choose, he decided he was going to choose Marie.

I tried to discuss it with him because I thought he was acting rashly. I didn't know what he was going to do instead and neither did he. It seemed impossible for him to just disappear overnight and live a normal life, not after all that he had been through and how many eyes were upon him. But he remained determined that things were going to change.

"I've given them enough of me! I've given them everything I have and now it's time to take something back for myself," he yelled.

"But you can't just give this all up. What are you going to do with your life? Are you really going to be happy just living without doing anything, without *singing*? What are you going to do?"

"I'm going to spend time with the woman I love, just the two of us. I'm going to end up with a family of my own and I won't have to worry about anyone interfering with my life. I can finally be left alone. I know I have a gift and there's a part of me that belongs to the world, but that doesn't mean I have to feed them all the time. I've given them myself. They have enough to sate their hunger."

Somehow, I knew that wasn't true. They would never stop wanting to gorge themselves on his song, his essence. But Drew was determined. He was waiting to tell Marie the good news when tragedy struck. People had always hated Marie for being so close with Drew, for occupying the space that they thought they deserved. They had tried to tempt Drew with their bodies, trying to pry him away from her, but when that didn't work, one of them decided to take matters into her own hands. Her name was Marie too and, in her twisted mind, she believed that she and Drew had been meant for each other; it just so happened that Drew's Marie had beaten her to the punch. One day, she walked up to Marie and shot her. It happened as quickly as a crack of thunder. There was no chance for Marie to plead for her life, no chance for the paramedics to save her. She had been shot through the heart.

We all had.

Marie DeVos was caught immediately. She had fallen to her knees and cackled, shouting that she could then be together with Drew. She was taken away and locked up, sentenced for life. But the punishment didn't help bring justice for Marie or closure for Drew. Marie DeVos even started a blog from prison where she talked about her devotion for Drew and how, in time, he would come to see that he loved her and that everything she had done had come from the heart. She had a surprising amount of followers considering her crime and her words always managed to worm their way out into the world despite her chilling actions.

When the news came, Drew collapsed. He was too numb to cry. It was one of those moments where reality seemed to blur into something unreal, where nothing seemed right and everything seemed wrong. We held each other as we tried to process things. We had been through so much together, but we had never experienced death before. I remember him shuddering in my arms. I remember the hoarse whispers and breaths that escaped his lips, the quiet pleas for salvation.

But there was no god to help him.

Marie had gone. There was no opportunity for him to say the things that had been on his mind. There was no chance to tell her that he was going to give it all up for her. She never knew that she was the most important person in the world to him. The sorrow was unbearable. We had never known pain like it and I almost lost him too. I gave him space because I thought it was what he needed. I tried to tell him that it would be okay, even though deep down I knew it wouldn't be. People were on at me for news, for a song, for anything, but I shut them down. This was Drew's time and I wouldn't have blamed him if he had used this opportunity to disappear.

But he didn't.

When I asked him if he was going to go, he said that he had nowhere to go to. The only reason he had wanted to leave this life was to be with Marie; without her, there was nothing keeping him here. He pulled himself up and went into the recording studio. He started a stream on a video site and sang songs for Marie, all the saddest, loveliest songs that he had ever known. From that moment, every song he sung was meant for her and nobody else. The deluded ones might believe that he was singing to them, but he was only singing to her.

*

"Drew, you can't keep doing this to yourself. I know it's painful, but you have to try and let her go."

"How can I let her go?" spittle flew from his mouth. His words were terse. "She was my life and she was taken from me. They took her from me." His hands closed into tight fists. In his darkest moods, he blamed his fans for her death even though it had only been the work of one woman. But, in a way, he was right. After all, legions of them had sniped Marie and told her that she wasn't good enough for Drew. They had tried to break the two of them up and while many of his fans had shown sympathy and joined in mourning, there were others who saw it as an opportunity. Some of the more wild ones had even undergone plastic surgery to look like Marie. The results were ghoulish.

Drew retreated from the world. The only time he showed any kind of emotion was when he was on stage; he always looked into the sky because he was looking up at Marie.

"If she was still around, I wouldn't have any of this. I was going to leave this all behind, Jamie. I could have had everything. Without her, all I have is the music. But now I...I find it more difficult to get up on that stage, to sing the same words over and over again when none of them really understand. None of them want me and my pain. None of them want to experience what it's like to lose the one they love. They just want me to make their lives better."

I nodded solemnly. None of them understood that a god could suffer.

"I thought that I was doing this for her, you know. I thought that if I kept singing somehow it would keep her spirit alive in the world. I guess that doesn't make much sense given how she always hated it. Maybe I should have given up a long time ago," Drew croaked, still with his head hanging down. He looked a pitiful figure. There were moments when I couldn't believe that this was the same person who had worn a fresh-faced look of awe in that first gig. Back then, we were both so innocent, unaware of how life could corrode and corrupt things, how a heart could be twisted into something dark and hopeless.

"She always loved the music, Drew. She just didn't like the fans and how much they wanted. She wouldn't have wanted you to stop singing."

"Maybe it is time though," Drew said. "I just... I can't imagine doing this for the rest of my life. I know that some people can. I can't. I've given them everything. I feel empty inside. Hollow. Every time I come off that stage, I feel drained, as though I have nothing left inside me. I worry that if I continue, I'm just going to end up giving everything until I end up dead. But maybe that's the only thing left for me to do, to leave everything behind. Then I can be anything they want me to be. It's not like I can do anything else. I'd just live in an empty house somewhere, surrounded by shadows and whispers and memories. What kind of a life is that?"

The question was rhetorical, but what Drew didn't know was that I had an answer for him.

*

The media companies who managed Drew's image wanted the funeral to be broadcast and streamed over the internet, but Drew vehemently disagreed with this. Fans had caused nothing but strife to Marie and he didn't want anything to get in the way of her peace and saying farewell to her. We had a simple funeral and we said our goodbyes. Her family was there, weeping at the tragedy. I don't think they blamed Drew for what happened, but he still blamed himself. In his mind, if he hadn't been famous, nobody would have targeted Marie, and she would have been able to live a long, happy life.

There was no eulogy spoken, but Drew did say a few words as he stood over her coffin. The coffin was sleek and black, and a picture of her and Drew stood upon it, when they were at their happiest. Tears flowed and I said goodbye as well. It seemed cruel that I should live when someone like Marie would die. I made a promise to her that I would do everything I could to make Drew happy.

The better part of a year passed. The days were long and Drew was a shell of himself, only coming alive when he performed. The fans couldn't see the toll this had all taken on him. They only saw him battling on like a warrior, still giving them what they wanted and needed. They repaid him with kindness. Bouquets of flowers arrived at his door. Donations were made to charities that Marie had supported. There was lots of love poured out to him and it was one of the few touching moments that fame brought. However, his condition didn't improve. I was concerned for him because he didn't let many people in. Marie had been the only other person to break through his defences and he shared things with her that he never could with me. I spent as much time with him as I could and tried to get him to open up about things, but I could sense that he was holding things back. It was only when he sang that he let everything out, all for her.

I was the only person who had known him before he had risen to fame. I was in a unique position to see that something was more than wrong. People saw his grief and isolation as being the eccentric quirks of an artist, rather than warning signs of a troubled soul. His work ethic was intact, but everything else, well, everything else was in jeopardy.

It was at this point when I had a meeting with a strange woman. She called me and said that she was from Veiled Truth, a company that specialised in the luxurious and niche needs of celebrities. I answered the phone sceptically, fearing that it was a scam, but the more she spoke, the more I thought she might be onto something. She expressed concern for Drew and asked me about his mental condition, rather than anything to do with his performances or his artistic output. After we had been speaking for a little while, she asked to meet me in person and I agreed, intrigued by what she had to say.

Evelyn Pickford was a tall, slender woman with pinched features and hair so blonde it was white, almost the same shade as her skin. She had a long face and sharp spectacles that rested on the bridge of her nose. She carried a black leather satchel with her and her heels made a rhythmic clacking sound as she walked. We met in an office I used to discuss various matters with people of importance. There was a coffee machine in the office, but Evelyn declined, preferring to drink filtered water. She had a clipped accent and every word was enunciated perfectly. I could imagine her being intimidating to anyone in a board room, but I was confident in my own skin and wasn't going to be swayed by anything she had to say, unless it was of interest to me or Drew.

"You said on the phone that you cater to the luxury needs of your clients. What exactly do you mean by that?" I asked. She had been rather vague on the phone, but what she said had been enough to capture my interest.

"We're aware that people of a certain level of fame cannot live like other people, nor should they. With their fame and wealth, there are certain things that a celebrity might wish that are usually beyond the realms of possibility or that might draw the attention of unscrupulous people looking to make a quick buck for selling a tawdry story. That is where we come in. We make all the arrangements. It's discreet and reliable, while privacy is respected at all times. There are no judgments."

I furrowed my brow and looked at her carefully. "Listen, Evelyn, I don't know what you think is happening here, but Drew doesn't have any of these 'niche' interests you're talking about. He's actually a pretty simple man when you get down to it. I don't know what you think we need, but I'm not sure we're going to buy what you're selling."

The corners of her mouth twitched and her thin lips curled into a smile. "Oh, but you haven't heard what I have to offer you yet," she said. "We have noticed that Drew has been having a difficult time lately. I was very sorry to hear of Marie's passing. She seemed like such a bright person. I'm sure that the world is a little dimmer now that her star is no longer shining."

"Now, listen here," my tone grew harsh and I jabbed a finger in her direction. "I don't know what you've got in mind, but Drew is not going to have some kind of escort. I've dealt with your kind before. He's not going to have an arranged marriage and he's not going to cavort with anyone you represent to give them a boost of fame. Drew isn't like that."

"I'm sure he's not," Evelyn raised her eyebrows and sipped her water. "I'm actually rather stunned at your reaction," she added. "I would never suggest anything like that. I fear you have misunderstood my intentions completely, as well as what Veiled Truth does. It takes a special kind of understanding to appreciate the emotional toll that a celebrity can be under. The common man cannot understand what it's like to have your privacy invaded, to have every word scrutinised, every action disseminated, to be judged every moment of your life without any regard for what it might mean. We know what it's like to have abuse flung at you, to have the eyes of the world upon you at all. We know what a toll it can take, just as we know what it's like to have someone so precious torn away."

My hand fell back to the table and I leaned forward, clasping my hands, tilting my head to listen to her more. Evelyn continued.

"You see, Jamie, we are in the business of making the lives of celebrities better. They are in a unique position in the world and, more often than not, they're unprepared for what this life entails. I have been reviewing Drew's life and it does not appear that he was raised in a showbiz environment, nor did he show any inclination to be in the industry."

I shook my head. "No, all he wanted to do was sing."

"Exactly! And I'm sure that when fame came to him, he was taken aback by what it all entailed. There are just no support systems in place for people who enter this level of society, so we seek to make their lives a little bit easier."

"Why didn't you come to us before? He sure could have used this kind of advice earlier," I asked harshly. Evelyn flashed me a calm smile.

"Even though our resources are vast, they are not infinite. We cannot help everyone," she said.

"And what makes you think Drew is in need of your help now?"

"We have been keeping an eye on him since Marie died. We have noticed how his behaviour has changed and how he seems to have lost his enjoyment of life. It is always sad when this happens and I would not want things to peter out like this. He still has much to offer. I can only imagine the mental toll that has been placed upon him after the death of Marie, especially because it came at the hands of one of his fans. Frankly, I don't know how he manages to get up on stage and still perform for them night after night, knowing that murder might lurk in their hearts."

"I think he tells himself that the person who shot Marie was an exception to the rule. Besides, he doesn't have much to live for other than his fans now. It's funny you should come along now, really. He was thinking of giving it all up before Marie died. But since she's gone, he doesn't think there's any other point to his existence. He's giving himself to his fans now, only living for them. He thinks that it's the only reason he's still here."

"And that is not a healthy state of mind at all. This is what we are concerned about. When artists reach a certain level of fame, the dependency on their fans can become as dangerous as their dependency on the celebrity. It can be very messy, especially when the celebrity loses a loved one. In Drew I see someone who is struggling and, as someone who has been by his side from the very beginning, I assume that you want the best for him?"

"I do," I said, still a little unsure about what she was getting at.

"Good, then you might be interested in this. It's a way for celebrities to leave their lives behind, to begin again and rediscover themselves. It's a way for them to be happy without feeling the demands placed upon them by their fans. I think Drew would be an ideal candidate and that his quality of life could be improved immeasurably." She seemed to be waiting for me to respond, but I was still unsure. Evelyn opened her satchel and plucked out a leaflet, sliding it across the table towards me. It was white, with a stark black picture of a sun rising over the horizon etched upon it.

"Tell me, Jamie," she continued, "do you think he will ever be happy if he continues performing for his fans?"

At the time, I didn't have an answer for her, even though I feared the truth that settled deep within my heart. I reached across the table and slid the leaflet towards me, gnawing my lower lip as I opened it.

*

As I looked at Drew sitting there so pitifully, I reached into my back pocket and pulled out the leaflet that had been sitting in there for months. I had intended to talk to him about it at some point, but there was always the hope that he would be able to pull himself out of his fugue state and begin to enjoy life again. I thought that at some point he might meet someone else to spark a new hope within him, but things had only deteriorated and I hated to see him like that.

But was Veiled Truth really the answer?

The question Evelyn had asked at the meeting had rattled around my mind ever since she had left the office.

Could I see Drew being happy if he continued like this?

At the time, I had lied to her and to myself by saying that of course he could. I had scoffed and quickly asked her to leave, but the question had lingered on my mind. I had clung to the best-case scenario for as long as possible before I came to the awful realisation that he would never be happy if I allowed this to continue. By giving himself to his fans, he was letting them leech off his emotions. He put so much of himself on stage that he never had anything else left when he was off it. He spent his free time staring into space or playing on his guitars, toying around with various pieces of music. There was no joy in his life at all and, as long as he lived only for his fans, that was not going to change.

I hated to be the one to say anything because he loved what the fans could give him, but I could see him crumbling before me, pieces of him falling away until there would be nothing left. Perhaps he should have died when Marie did; at least then they would have been at peace together and perhaps they could both live together in whatever lies beyond this mortal realm.

I cleared my throat before I spoke.

"Drew, there is something that might help, something that might free you of this."

"Free me? You speak as though I am a prisoner," Drew said with a wry smile. He may not have worn them, but I could see the chains that shackled him.

"I think we both know that you can't keep going like this, Drew. You've given your fans so much and they might give you plenty back as well, but you can't only live for them. It's not healthy, and it's not something that Marie would want."

Drew glared at me through the straggling hair, a sneering look turning his face ugly. "If you're going to try and tell me that I need to get out there and meet someone, you can just leave right now. I've already told you that I'm not going to fall in love with anyone again. She was the only one for me and I don't care if you say that it can just be something casual. I know people always expect me to find someone else, but there *is* no one else, so you can stop right there."

"I wasn't going to say that at all actually. There's something else. A while back, this woman came to see me. She's from a company called Veiled Truth. They take care of celebrities."

"What do you mean, '*They take care of them*'?"

"They provide services that celebrities will appreciate. She was quite convincing actually. She said that she understands the toll placed upon your mind and that you're not alone. There are others, many others who have suffered from similar things. You were never given the guidance on how to cope with this life and all it entails. All you want to do is sing. They want to help you, Drew. I should have come to you with this before, but I was hoping that you would be able to pull yourself out of this funk. You're only getting worse though. I have to be honest with you. I don't see anything good happening if you keep living like this. It's like you only appear when your fans want you to appear, as though you're some kind of genie dancing to their whims."

"What else is there?"

"You can live," I hissed and moved closer towards him. "If you just look at this, you can see how you can live and be free. You can experience life without being hounded by your fans, without having to be beholden to them. You wouldn't have to do anything you don't want to. You can just be free to live and breathe without the noose of your fans hanging around your neck."

Drew pursed his lips and breathed in deeply. "And what do they want for this?"

I averted my gaze and arched an eyebrow. "They want you to die," I said.

*

When I read through the leaflet I thought Evelyn was crazy. This whole thing seemed bizarre and surreal. I wasn't going to subject Drew to it. There was still a chance for him. He was still grieving, but I figured that once he had worked through his grief, it would all be better again. Evelyn didn't take offence at my refusal, but insisted that she would still be there, waiting, if I should ever change my mind. She reminded me that it was for Drew's benefit and that he might feel differently should I present it to him. I vowed that I wouldn't though. Drew wasn't in the right state of mind and I didn't want him to make a decision he would later regret. I didn't want him turning his back on everything he knew because of his emotional distress.

However, I didn't throw the leaflet away. Perhaps I should have, but I wanted it there as a way out in case things didn't improve. I feared in my heart that Evelyn was right, that Drew would never be able to shake this gloomy outlook on the world and, if he did, then perhaps dying was the only way to go.

*

"They want me to *die*?" Drew's face twisted in confusion and disbelief. He ran his hand through his hair again and leaned back in his chair, showing the patchwork illustrations that had been tattooed into his torso. "What the hell is this, Jamie? Are you trying to get me involved in a cult? I'm not going to fall for this crap if you're going to try and tell me that death is an escape and all we need to do is embrace the inevitable to be free. You should know better than that."

"I do, believe me, I do. Look," I folded the leaflet and put it back into my pocket. "When I spoke to them, they explained to me that there have been a lot of people who felt the same way as you. A lot of celebrities just couldn't take it; they became famous because of their talent, but that didn't make them better than other people or more worthy of this attention. This rise of celebrity was a phenomenon that few people could anticipate. The fanaticism and obsession that was conjured in these people was beyond comprehension and it led to a lot of celebrities struggling with mental health problems and committing suicide or becoming addicted to drugs as a way to cope with all the things they could not cope with. People started to realize that it wasn't going to be possible to continue like this, that celebrities needed help. But, too often, these people were reluctant to open up about their problems as that would have made them human and a fallible god wasn't one worth worshipping. People didn't want to hear about their heroes struggling with the same problems that they struggled with. They only wanted to hear stories larger than life and feel as though, with the right bit of luck, they could become celebrities too.

It all started with Elvis. He struggled more than most and, by the end, he couldn't take it anymore. It had cost him his marriage, his freedom. Eventually, he became a prisoner going from concert to concert, barely able to understand what was happening next. Everything had been taken from him, even the love for music and he knew it was going to kill him if he continued. He had to break free. He decided to die, at least the part of him that the fans knew. In reality, he disappeared to a tropical island, the location of which is a closely guarded secret and it's remained that way all these years. If fame gets too much for a celebrity to handle, they can leave everything behind and reclaim their life in a tropical, peaceful paradise."

Drew looked at me for a few moments and then scoffed, shaking his head.

"Whoever this woman is, she's really fed you something. You actually believe this? Come on, Jamie, if someone was going to choose how they died, why would they say they died while taking a crap? Give Elvis a little more credit than that."

"To make it more believable. Nobody is going to question him dying in such an embarrassing way and yet still people have. He left them his legacy, but he took his life. You can do the same. Come on, Drew, without Marie you've been so miserable and you haven't been able to do anything to bring you out of this daze. You go from day to day in a blur and there's no joy other than what you get when you're on the stage."

"Which is why this whole thinking is flawed!" Drew threw his hands up in exasperation. "If I'm only alive on stage, then why do you want to take me from it? Do you want me to be a ghost?"

"No, Drew, that's not what I'm saying at all. What I want is for you to be happy again. I want you to feel content with who you are. If everything you are comes from some external source, then what are you going to do when it all fades away? What's going to be left? At least this way you can break free of all this fame and live without worrying about what everyone else thinks of you. You won't have to put up with people sending you unsolicited pictures or marriage proposals, you won't have anyone declaring their undying love for you. You can just live by yourself without all of this noise going on. You can actually relax for once in your life."

My words were impassioned and Drew didn't dismiss the idea entirely.

"Alright, how does this work then?" he asked.

"They work with you to figure out how you're going to die. A drug overdose is usually the easiest because then you can get pictures of you as a corpse and generally people don't ask questions. Plus the pinpricks of your arm add to the evidence, although rather than being given any illegal drugs, you'll be sedated until they take you to their facility. Once there, you'll be woken up and transferred to a private jet where you'll be flown to the island. You'll live out your days in peace and luxury, where the sun always shines. I know it's not exactly like the life you imagined for yourself, surrounded by children in a cosy home, but at least you can find peace again. I just... I'm not sure how much longer I can go seeing you like this. When Marie died, I promised her that I would make sure you were happy. I'm not sure I've done a good job of keeping that vow. I thought that you could find your way back to your heart through your music, but you never seem to get any better. You just seem lost and I can't keep watching you die before my eyes. I want you to be happy again. I want you to be free of all this. Please, Drew, you've given them enough. They'll be fine without you. You can leave now. You can be free."

Drew still looked uncertain, but he sighed eventually and said that he would think about it. I suppose that was all I could ask. It was a lot to ask him to give up all of this when it was the only thing he had, but I hoped that he would see that it was for his own good. I could almost see him fading away as he sat there. A part of me wished we had never begun this journey at all.

*

It was a cold winter's night when Drew died. The wind was icy and bitter. Breath swirled and curled, rising through the air until it dissipated into nothingness. The news reports that came out, inspired by a statement I gave, declared that Drew had died of a drug overdose. It was reported that he had been suffering from grief and depression, and that he had never truly gotten over the loss of his wife. All those who knew him spoke about how he had seemed like a shadow of his former self after she had died, except when he was on stage. Then, they said, he was a force of nature.

Tributes poured in from all over the world and from millions of souls that Drew had touched. His songs were played over and over again, and vigils were held all over the world, but most notably in his hometown. Tears were wept and people declared that there would never be anyone like him to walk the earth again. I grieved too, and it wasn't an act, even though I knew that Drew wasn't really dead. But, in a way, he was. I would never get to see him again. It was a one-way trip to the island and it was only meant for the true elite level of celebrities that could afford the mind-boggling price.

In a lonely and cold jail cell, an alarm was raised as a guard walked by and saw a woman hanging from a rope cord. Her eyes bulged out of her head and her tongue lolled from her mouth. She had left a note, saying that she had killed herself so that she and Drew could be together in the afterlife. Marie

DeVos said that she would chase his soul wherever it went, because Drew was her destiny.

I didn't mourn her at all.

Unlike Marie's funeral, Drew's was a huge affair. People descended upon the chapel and blocked the streets for miles. It was streamed online and broke records for viewing figures. It was at times like these when I was truly awestruck by the impact Drew had had. To me, he was still the slightly awkward boy who didn't even realize he had the voice of an angel. I could picture him sitting in his bedroom, singing, while I recorded him on my phone. Back then, it was all so simple and neither of us could have seen where it was going to end. Even though only five years had passed since that day, it felt as though a lifetime had happened. He had fallen in love and then into grief. He had given so much of himself and had taken only a sliver back.

And what of me? I had spent those five years by his side, working diligently to ensure that Drew remained a star. I had sacrificed a lot myself as well. While Drew had found love, it had always eluded me.

While he basked in the adulation of his screaming fans, I had stood by the side, hidden in the shadows, wondering what it would be like to be a star. I suppose I would never know though, but at least I had helped him move on from this world. At least I had helped him to a better place. I could console myself in the knowledge that I had been a good friend and that ultimately I had kept the vow I had made to Marie. I knew that wherever Drew was, he was happier than he would have been here and, as I stood over his pretend casket, a tear rolled down my cheek.

*

Drew stepped off the plane, feeling a little dazed. The sun was bright and he had to shield his eyes. The sand was soft. The island beckoned him. A verdant mountain rose through the air and was framed by palm trees. A crystal blue sea lapped against the alabaster shore, the sand so bright it seemed to glow. People were dotted along the beach, sunning themselves, sipping cocktails. A murmur of relaxed chatter rose through the air and a bird chirped in the distance. There were few clouds in the sky. It was an idyllic place, certainly living up to the billing that Jamie had given it.

Drew's head dropped a little as he thought about his old friend. Jamie had always looked out for him and it was sad that they would never get to see each other again. Drew had lost everyone close to him and he was still unsure if he was going to find what he was looking for here. Still, it was probably too late to have misgivings like that considering there was no way back for him. He wouldn't have been able to return to his other life even if he wanted to.

Jamie had looked out for him even when he hadn't been able to look out for himself. Jamie had seen the toll his life was taking on him and for this Drew was grateful, because he had been blind. But the sun could not burn away his grief, at least not instantly. The only other thing he missed was the chanting of the crowd. It had been such a constant presence in his life for so long now that he trembled at the thought of never hearing it again. He closed his eyes and shuddered, realizing that Jamie was right. If he had such a hard time going without it, then perhaps it wasn't good for him.

"Hey, man, welcome to our little slice of paradise. I know it's not too original, but I call it Graceland," a man said, drawling. His voice sounded familiar and yet it seemed impossible. Drew looked up to see a man approaching him. He walked with a swagger, although the swagger was diminished and supported by a cane. A shock of white hair was slicked back around a handsome face, which was lined with soft wrinkles. Kind eyes twinkled and his smile was wide. He wore a flowing cloak that was clasped together with a lightning bolt brooch and ornate rings sat upon his fingers.

Drew had to blink a few times before he realised who he was seeing.

"Elvis?" he gasped.

"The one and only," Elvis replied. Drew thought this was impossible. Surely the man should have been dead by now.

"I know what you're thinking, son," Elvis said, "I should be dead by now. Well, maybe I should be, but this place is good for the soul. As long as the soul has energy, you ain't ever gonna die. Now then, let me get you settled in. Back there is where you're going to stay. Your room is already prepared. We've got everything you could ever want to be happy..." Elvis' voice trailed off as Drew tried to understand what was happening. He was actually standing there with Elvis, being shown paradise. It was better than he could have ever imagined and all the doubts started to vanish from his mind.

"Oh, and there's someone else here who is eager to meet you," Elvis chuckled slightly and gestured with his cane to the far side of the beach. He nudged Drew forward, humming an old tune as he did so. Drew peered towards the beach and walked towards it, the sand slipping through his toes. The heat had a little bite to it, but not enough to make things uncomfortable.

The figure that Elvis had pointed to seemed familiar, even from a distance. She had coppery hair that came down to her waist and she wore a red bikini. As Drew approached, she turned to face him and smiled, a smile that stretched across her beautiful heart-shaped face. She ran towards him kicking up sand as she did so, much to the annoyance of people around her. She flung her arms around his neck and peppered him with kisses, leaving him in a daze.

"Marie?" he leaned back and placed his arms around her hips. Even though he was looking into her eyes and touching her waist, he couldn't actually believe this was her.

"It's me, Drew. God, I'm so sorry that this had to happen. I'm sorry that I couldn't tell you."

"Tell me what? How are you here? What's going on?"

"It's okay," she clasped his hand and smiled the same smile that had always set his mind at ease, even in his most troubled moments. "Veiled Truth came to me a while back. They had seen all the awful messages and treatment I was getting and the strain it was putting on our relationship. They told me that I could be free of it, that there was a way for us to be together. All I had to do was fake my death. They got to Marie first, gave her a gun with blanks in it. She was too crazy to check. All I had to do was lie to you. Drew, I'm so sorry for everything I've put you through. I never wanted it to be like this. Leaving you behind was the hardest thing I ever had to do. And lying to you... Oh, God...I can't imagine what it's been like for you. I'm sorry. I'm so sorry."

Her voice cracked with emotion as she pulled him into her. Drew closed his eyes and breathed in the familiar scent that he had pined for. He ran his hands along her back and played with the ends *of her hair, feeling the warmth of her body and her heartbeat. A part of him was afraid this was a trick, but no, nobody could feel the way she did. He knew her more than he knew anything else and, even though it seemed impossible, he knew that she was in his arms once again. Her hair flowed through his fingers like coppery ribbons. Her soft cheeks pressed against his. Her breath, the sweet warmth of her lips, the sparkle of her eyes... It was all there before him. He didn't care that this was impossible. The gnawing doubt at the back of his mind was pushed back by the overwhelming joy he felt at being with her again, at feeling this utter joy and happiness. All the anguish that had swelled within him suddenly disappeared and he felt more complete than he had done for longer than he could remember.*

"Why didn't you tell me, Marie?" he asked, his voice choking on the pain. All this time he had been grieving, she had been here.

"I know, I'm sorry, I just couldn't take it. They approached me and talked to me about what they could offer. The plan was for you to join me, but you took longer. But it's okay. You're here now. We're together again and we don't have to worry

about anything. Oh, Drew, it's wonderful here. You're going to love it."

She linked hands with him and squeezed tightly while she smiled. Dimples appeared on her cheek and she kissed him again. Drew didn't care that this shouldn't be happening. He didn't care that this went against everything he believed to be true. The only thing that mattered was that she was standing before him. He smiled and nodded.

"Then I guess you'd better show me around," he smirked. Marie's eyes lit up with delight and she beamed, beginning to tell him about all the things the island could offer. Freed of the demands of their fans, they could finally live the life they had always wanted. They walked across the soft sand and disappeared into the trees as above them the sun curved across the world.

*

I stood before Drew's casket, my hand on the dark shell.

"So, he really won't know what's happening?" I asked. Evelyn emerged from the shadows behind me.

"Not at all. He came here right after he was sedated. He won't know a thing. As far as he knows, he's on the island with all the others.

I even programmed in the special surprise you asked for. It's lucky you knew her so well. We were able to create a genuine illusion of her."

I nodded sombrely. A lump formed in my throat. "I just hope he doesn't realize the truth."

"Even if he does, he'll dismiss it as simple paranoia. The thing is, Jamie, people believe what they want to believe. They create a reality that makes sense to them. Drew will be willing to accept this world we've created for him because it makes him happy. People want that more than they want the truth. You've given him a great gift, the gift of freedom. He'll never know misery again."

"But it's not really *life*, is it?" I said, beginning to have second thoughts, even though I knew it was pointless because this was a one-way trip.

Evelyn offered a thin smile. "Life is whatever we make it. The illusion is believing that we have to accept reality even if it makes us miserable. You saved him. If Drew had continued down that path, he would have been swallowed by his own misery. The same is true for the rest of them." As Evelyn said this, she gestured to the other cubicles that were held in these chambers. Jamie looked up in awe at the number of them. There were so many people who had retreated here and were now housed in these chambers. Nutrients were injected and dripped directly into their system, while they remained in a virtual world. A virtual reality headset hid their faces from view, while special equipment was housed inside the casket to stimulate tactile responses, making Drew believe that he really was on a tropical island with Marie. It had been my final parting gift to him, a way to make sure that he was genuinely happy. I knew that she was the only thing that could bring him true peace.

"You don't have to feel guilty. I can assure you that all of these people are happier than they would have been if they stayed in this world. We monitor their brainwaves. None of them have ever expressed any desire to leave."

I nodded, ignoring the doubt and guilt that nagged at me. I told myself that he had always been a prisoner, trapped by his fame. At least now he could pretend to be free. This was the only way he could have some kind of life. There were so many others as well, all experiencing their personal paradise after being hounded and dogged by fame, after having all their privacy torn away from them.

"So, what happened to the actual island then?" I asked.

Evelyn placed her hands together, forming the shape of a steeple. "Unfortunately, the lure of escaping their life proved too popular and the island became crowded. The more people that became involved, the greater chance there was of the secret being revealed. With this set-up, we can help more people. He's given enough to the world, Jamie. Let him be at peace now," she said.

I nodded and bid my final farewell to my dear friend. I left the bland skyscraper and walked back home. As cars passed by, I heard Drew's songs on the radio. His videos were still being played on TV screens in stores as I walked through the city. People wore t-shirts of him and styled their hair like him. They still posted messages on his website and commented on his old videos, mourning him, sharing their love for him. He had touched so many people in the world, but there was only so much adulation a man could take. We weren't built to be gods, to be worshipped. At least he was in a better place now. Maybe sometimes people need a lie more than they need the truth.

Seek and Hide

Dr. Sirius Endecol was a thin man with glossy black hair that was swept back into a mane. His features were pale and gaunt and, to most people, he was unassuming and they wouldn't recognize him at all if they passed him on the street. But, to others, he was the most important man in the world and, to some, he may well have been the most important man in history.

Dr. Endecol had spent his entire life searching for the unknown. Ever since he was a child, he had been fascinated by the endless mystery of the universe. As the years had gone by and men had developed newer and more powerful technology, the layers of the universe had been peeled back. More planets had been scanned, black holes had been mapped, the galaxy had been chartered in a way that gave humanity a good sense of the area in which they lived. And yet, despite their vast knowledge of the galaxy, there was still one thing missing; the experience.

In 2330 AD, humanity was still a species of dreamers. Despite many efforts to develop faster-than-light technology in order to traverse the vast distances in the cosmos, all the efforts had failed. Sirius knew that they would always fail and that something else was needed to be done. After winning his Nobel Prize, he sat down with a reporter from the Germanic Herald, the most highly read newspaper in the world, although that wasn't difficult considering Germanic territory spanned the whole of what used to be called Europe and most of what used to be Russia too. Matilda von Beauchamp was a beautiful woman and an acclaimed journalist. She had blonde hair that was neatly trimmed and a slender frame. One eye glowed as the cybernetic implant shifted into recording mode and, as Sirius sat down for his interview, he smiled and shook her hand. In her eyes he saw something of the same spark that he recognized in his younger self and he was filled with a sense of longing. His life had had one focus – one direction – and, as a result, he had missed out on so many other things that other people experienced in their lifetime. She wore a burgundy suit and smiled politely, relaxing into her chair.

"Dr. Endecol, it's a pleasure to meet you," she said in a lilting accent, a fascinating blend of English, German and French.

"Please, call me, Sirius," the doctor said, nodding. Matilda inclined her head in response.

"I first want to begin by congratulating you on this most impressive achievement. Many have claimed that you have done the impossible and that even a Nobel Prize is not enough to celebrate your accomplishments. As you sit here today, can you actually believe that you did this or does it feel like a dream?"

Sirius laughed. "I have to admit that I have been pinching myself more often than not lately, but this has been something I've spent my whole life working on and even though at times it felt like it was never going to happen, I'm not one to doubt the truth. But thank you for your kind words."

"You're welcome. What was it exactly that made you eschew traditional wisdom and research something other than faster-than-light travel?"

"Well, it was a combination of things really. When I was a child, I was fascinated by the stars; I always used to look up at them. My mother often sat up with me at night and told me everything she knew about them. Then, I started learning about the efforts made to travel the stars and I was disheartened. Like so many others, I was traumatised when I heard about the space races of the late 21st century. I didn't understand how the different governments could see it as a competition, trying to undermine each other, and the last thing I wanted was to incite another war. Looking back at the history of the space program, even going back to its inception in the 20th century, it has always been plagued by this competitive edge. Even though travelling through space is a worthy goal, I wasn't sure it warranted all the destruction that came with it. And then there are the disasters that have torn up chunks of the world because people have been experimenting with nuclear fission and other unstable energy. In my humble opinion, going to the stars shouldn't result in the destruction of our own planet.

I went to many conferences and seminars, and one of the main topics was how we were going to fight the legislation that prevented using certain materials, because it was assumed that an engine powerful enough to carry a space craft away from earth, breaking through our atmosphere, was the only way we were going to travel through space. Frankly, I couldn't believe my ears. These people, these *scientists*, were spending more time cutting through red tape than they were in trying to make actual progress. I have always thought that the beauty of science is the way it can adapt to changing circumstances and how we, as scientists, need to open our minds to new possibilities. When I looked at all the available information, it was clear that people were so wedded to the idea of using an engine to fly through the stars that they couldn't think of anything else. So, I decided that I would try to find an alternative."

"It was that easy?" Matilda asked, arching an eyebrow.

Sirius chuckled. "Oh, no, this was a decision that took many months of anguish. It was something that went against the accepted wisdom of my brethren. After all, every time we've moved humans anywhere we have used some form of locomotion, but there was one form of travel that had always fascinated me – ships. I looked to the sea and I realized that long ago, before we had the huge cruise cities, people used to take boats out that had no engines. They used the currents of the water to carry them and, while it was slow, it meant that could traverse vast distances without having any advanced technology. I thought the same might be true for space as well."

"So, by looking into the past, you actually managed to see a way to progress in the future?"

"Yes!" Sirius said excitedly. "I thought of how an ancient person would have stood on his shore and looked out at the ocean, wondering about what lay beyond the horizon. In many ways, we hadn't changed at all, except the sea is now the stars and the shore is our own atmosphere. We have had the ability to break free of gravity for a long time, but it takes up so much fuel we're practically dead in space once we're up there. I wondered if there wasn't something we were missing. Had we spent so much time focused on flying through space that we had missed something vital? Had we been looking at the wrong area? Once I started to ask myself those questions, the process seemed quite natural to me and everything followed from there."

"But you were met with strong opposition, weren't you, and it was difficult for you to receive funding?"

"Yes," Sirius scratched his chin and sighed as he thought of those days. "I was trying to do something that went against accepted wisdom, so of course people thought that I was wasting my time and going to naturally fail. I had to beg and do as many favours as possible for people just to get them to listen to me. I had a small office and very few people wanted to work with me as they thought it was a flyway to nowhere. I had a ragtag team and, in truth, I didn't even know what I was looking for. I was just looking out there, hoping that I would discover something like a current that would carry our ships through the stars."

"Tell me, what was it like when you first discovered a wormhole?"

"Well, it was the best day of my life. It seemed like the concept with the most potential, but actually finding the kind of wormholes we needed was proving challenging. We could detect them, but that wasn't enough. We had to be able to chart them and look through them; we had to make sure that they were stable."

"How did you even come up with the idea to look for wormholes?" Matilda asked, a look of awe upon her soft features. Sirius blushed and rubbed the back of his neck.

"Actually, that's something that I should confess. I can't make myself out as this grand visionary who was five steps ahead of everyone. I had a dozen different potential avenues to explore and it just so happened that we hit on wormholes. But it did take thorough research to come to that conclusion.

Sometimes perseverance is more impressive than inspiration," he smiled wryly. "But, of course, the next challenge was to develop new technology to sense these wormholes. Thankfully, people were starting to take me more seriously, so I had access to more resources and I was able to develop the Endescope, which allowed us to inspect the stability of a wormhole and the likely length."

"And now we can use wormholes to chart the stars," Matilda said.

"Indeed! They have been there all along, just waiting for us to use them. We just need enough fuel to get us to the first wormhole. Then we can chart a path using different wormholes to pull the craft along. It's all very exciting. We have tested the process with probes and the results have been positive. It opens up the galaxy for us and the possibilities are endless! It's a very exciting time to be alive and I'm grateful that I can be here to experience it."

"As am I, doctor... I mean Sirius," Matilda said, blushing. "And can you give me your thoughts on the Horizon project?"

"Well, I think it's just wonderful. The wonderful thing about the scientific community is that once a new idea is presented and it has evidence behind it, they're ready to throw their weight into exploring it. People were eager to utilise the wormholes and we're ready to take our bow on the galactic stage. This is going to be the most important event in human history and I can't fathom what we're going to find out there. To think of all the unexplored planets there are and that's not even mentioning the different species we might meet!"

"Are you convinced there are aliens? Throughout the history of humanity, there has not been any proof of alien contact."

"Well, that's not strictly true. There was the Luma signal, even though I know there is much controversy surrounding that. One man's white noise is another man's alien transmission, or so the saying goes," Sirius chuckled at his own joke. "But if there is life out there, we finally have the chance to make contact. I feel as though humanity has been poised for this moment for centuries now and we've been so eager to take this step that we've almost stumbled, but we're finally ready."

"And it's all thanks to you," Matilda bowed her head. "And what is next for you, Sirius? Do you have any other projects in mind or is changing humanity once in your lifetime enough for one man?"

Sirius smiled, but that smile faded when he thought about the question. His brow crinkled and he averted his gaze. "Actually, you know, I haven't given much thought to what's coming next. I shall follow the progress of the Horizon, but after that..." For a moment, he lost himself in a strange feeling of melancholy. For so long, he had been sure of his purpose. His life had revolved around his research and the thrill of the chase to develop this technology. Even in the bleakest moments, it had still been exhilarating because he had been striving for something, but now he was faced with the possibility of doing nothing. "I'm not quite sure," he added.

Matilda declared that she had enough for her piece and that it had been a pleasure. She rose, but lingered for a moment. "Sirius, I wondered if I might trouble you for a drink later. There are many more things I would like to talk about with you, *off the record*," she smiled shyly and tilted her head to the side, gently rolling her lower lip underneath her teeth. Sirius nodded and said that he would be happy to. It was never a chore to spend time talking about his work, so they agreed to meet a little later on. However, Sirius had to make one thing clear.

"You realize that I can't give you any information about the Horizon project. Until we get the go-ahead from our superiors, it's strictly confidential."

"Oh, I know. Don't worry, Sirius! I'm not going to make you do anything you don't want to do. Can't a girl just want to spend time with the most brilliant man on the planet?" she caressed his arm before she walked away and gave him the most enigmatic look. Sirius cleared his throat and clearly felt his cheeks redden. He pursed his lips and wondered if she was joking or not.

*

The Horizon project was a global coalition where the Pacific States, Germanic

Territories, the Asian Coalition, the African Collection and New America had combined to show a unified front in this most hallowed effort to take humanity to the stars once again. There was much excitement about what they might find and a noted crew of the most talented astronauts and scientists had been assembled to man the Horizon and go to space. Led by Grace Chung, the crew were going to be the heroes and the faces of this new era of space travel, and Sirius was certain that they were going to inspire a generation of children.

There was a little part of him that gnawed with envy. It was his role in history to find a way to travel the stars, but not to travel them himself. He was not strong or fit enough for that, and unless great strides were made in his lifetime to increase the comfort of space travel and make it more accessible for average people, he would always be fated to stare up at the stars rather than fly through them. Still, as a scientist, he recognized that his role in life wasn't to experience everything, but to be a stepping stone for progress and to guide humanity in the right direction.

He watched the crew assemble and make their speeches. It was being broadcast all over the world. He smiled when they made mention of his name. It was still hours until the shuttle would launch, so he went to meet Matilda at the bar in the meantime.

*

When he arrived, he saw her immediately. She dressed in a loose top that was cut low and left one shoulder exposed. Her skin was flawless and her smile intoxicating. Her face lit up when she saw him and she led him to a small booth. They tapped on the menu on the table to order the drinks and Matilda pressed her wrist to the menu to pay.

"Oh, thank you, you didn't have to do that," Sirius said.

"It's my pleasure. Thank you for joining me. I'm sorry that things were so formal earlier. I'm glad to be able to relax," she said, fluttering her eyelashes. He noticed that her cybernetic implant wasn't glowing and he breathed a sigh of relief. Perhaps it was paranoid of him, but he didn't understand why a woman such as her would want to spend time with him if she wasn't getting anything out of it. "I watched the broadcast earlier. It's all so exciting, isn't it? I wonder what those people are feeling, knowing that their names are going to go 'up' in history. I'd love to be on that ship."

"As would I, but they're very capable of handling everything and earth couldn't ask for better representatives."

"You mean if they meet aliens? Do you think it's really possible?"

A robot waiter came over and served their drinks. Sirius felt the taste of the synthehol and enjoyed the hazy feeling from the colourful drink. He couldn't believe that people would actually imbibe liquid that would harm their insides.

"I like to think so. I hate to think that we're alone in this world. When you think of how many worlds there are and how many possibilities... it makes me think that it's impossible for us to not be alone."

"But surely we would have experienced contact before this?" Matilda asked.

"I'm not sure. You know, one thing that we didn't touch on in the interview is that this technology allows us to scan the universe in real time rather than rely on images that come from millions and billions of years in the past. It's not a far cry to say that we have never had an accurate picture of our universe, so we might well have missed something obvious."

"So, you think that perhaps there are aliens out there and we just haven't seen them because we never got to that point in history yet?"

"Exactly. But there are other reasons why aliens might not have made contact too."

"I know the theories. One is that aliens see us as undeveloped; another is that we're too far away from the main galactic highway. I suppose it's difficult to put ourselves into the minds of an alien race. Wouldn't it be sad if we were the only species in the universe that wanted to connect with other species? It would be like being at a party with a bunch of strangers and nobody is saying anything."

"You know, I think I've been to a few parties like that in my time," Sirius admitted.

"Me too," Matilda laughed and arched her head back as she took a long sip of her drink. The fluted glass was as slender as her neck and Sirius caught himself gazing at the hollow of her throat. He thought that they must have improved the formula for synthehol as it was having a more intense reaction than it ever had done before.

"I really feel like we're on the cusp of something amazing," Matilda continued, "and it's all thanks to you. I just...I can't believe that I'm actually with you right now. It's crazy," she leaned forward and her lips glistened. There was a sultry look in her eyes and her hand rested against his arm. Sirius smiled and nodded. "You know, to prepare for the interview today I did a little research on you. How come you never had a family?"

"Well, you see, it never seemed very feasible. I spent so much time on my work that I knew I would never be able to give someone my full attention. The only way would have been to sacrifice my research, but I knew that it was important to the human race to continue. I made a choice to delay looking for a wife, then my research took longer and longer, and then, I suppose, the opportunity just slipped away."

"But don't you get lonely?"

"I suppose I do at times, but I'm used to living life like this and I've never believed that anyone should depend on anyone but themselves for happiness."

"Well, no, but there's a lot more you can get from someone else."

"I'm sure there is, but a long time ago I made peace with the fact that not everyone is going to get to experience everything in their lifetime. I have a Nobel Prize and if that means I had to sacrifice human companionship, then so be it. I'm sure that you've managed to find a nice balance though. Someone like you must have no shortage of companions."

Matilda laughed a throaty laugh and smiled widely. "It's true, I'm only lonely when I want to be, but there's something more, something I've always craved and I haven't met the right man yet. I'm just surprised that nobody has snapped you up. Intelligence is very sexy you know."

"It is? I never got that memo," Sirius replied, smiling. Matilda laughed and sidled closer to him. He could feel her hand rise up his arm. The air was alive with her fragrant scent and the rest of the world drifted away into murmurs as she became the only thing in his vision, vivid and bright. Breath caught in his throat and his heart hammered. This shouldn't have been happening. This kind of thing was a game for the young. It had all passed him by. He had sacrificed this for the sake of his work. He had condemned himself to a life of loneliness and he had come to terms with that willingly, but now…now there was a possibility for more.

She leaned in and spoke in a breathy whisper.

"I hope this isn't unprofessional of me, but I'd love to get a little closer to you and pick your brains about…oh…*everything*," her voice descended into a throaty laugh again and Sirius felt his insides curdle. He swallowed the lump of uncertainty that swelled in his throat and nodded.

"I'm sure that could be arranged," he said. Matilda giggled and leaned into him. She fawned over him for the rest of the night as they spoke about a range of topics and he relaxed in her company. The time flew by as they discussed history, the politics of the word, and delved into their own personal dreams and inspirations. Sirius found himself sharing things with her that he had not spoken about with anyone before and it was thrilling. He was entirely lost in her company and lost all track of time, as did she apparently, for they were both surprised when the robo waiter came by to tell them that the bar was closing. They walked out into the fresh air of the night. Matilda glowed as brightly as a star. Her cybernetic implant flashed as she ordered a cab to take her home.

"Well, tonight was lovely and I do hope we meet again," Sirius said. His words were suffocated in a passionate kiss. Matilda flung herself at him and pinned him against a wall. Her lips were soft and tender, yet ardent. Her shapely body melted into his and it felt as though a wall crumbled all around him. There had been so much he had denied himself in life and so much he thought he would never have. Matilda left as her cab pulled up, but Sirius remained, feeling stunned. He relaxed against the wall and felt a dazed, dreamy look come over him before he made his way home, unable to wipe the smile from his face. It felt as though the world was finally falling into place. There were possibilities at home and possibilities in the stars. And yet, still, he was plagued with the question of what came next.

Was a history project enough for one man? Could Sirius rest on his laurels or was there something else waiting for him? Did he have the energy to pour into another project that would change the world or had he earned retirement? He had been working so hard for so long that the thought of retiring was anathema to him and yet, what else was left for him? He would not be able to go into the stars, nor would he be able to make first contact with alien species. The government had diplomatic specialists for that. As far as the governments of the world were concerned, his part in exploring the stars was largely over. They didn't even really need him to work the technology. It was almost as though he was a spare part.

*

Sirius was in the control room as the Horizon prepared for launch. The excitement of the previous night still made his heart beat powerfully. While there were doubts about his future, he wasn't going to let them affect his performance and he wasn't going to let himself drown in melancholy. Like all things, this would pass, and he was determined to enjoy the sight of humanity exploring a new region of the stars. Using the Endescope, they had charted a path through wormholes that would take them far beyond the solar system to unknown worlds. Everyone was bubbling with excitement and it was a joy to be a part of this, to feel the energy surging around the room. Sirius listened to the excited musings and the wary concerns. Some were worried about what the Horizon might find out there in the farthest reaches of space. The probes hadn't detected anything dangerous, but if they were to meet alien life, there was always the chance that they might be hostile. There was also the possibility that, just as at sea, there were grisly creatures that spelled doom for any unsuspecting travellers. But still, that was a part of the excitement. The Horizon was equipped with the most advanced sensors and would record as much information as possible on its trip through the wormholes.

"Horizon to base. We're clear for take-off. I hope your calculations are correct. The last thing I want is to be drifting out there in the unknown," Grace Chung said over a transmission. All eyes turned to Sirius, who gave them a reassuring smile. There was no doubt in his mind that the Endescope would find a path through the currents of space and bring them back home without any trouble at all.

"Captain Chung, there are going to be no problems at all. We look forward to your transmission when you're in space. You are a go for launch," the man in charge of the launch said. Sirius watched on a monitor as the Horizon fired its engines and soared into the sky, ascending like an angel to heaven. Smoke billowed out in a cloud and the mission was underway.

The control room was filled with tension as they waited for news from the Horizon. On their monitors they could see the Horizon break through the atmosphere and enter space. Grace Chung's voice came over the communication, detailing every step of their movement. Sirius waited with bated breath as the Horizon moved to the entry point of a wormhole. Even though there was nothing theoretically different between a probe and a shuttle, it still felt different because the Horizon was filled with people.

"There might be a momentary delay in transmission," control told the astronauts.

"Preparing to thrust in 3...2...1," Captain Chung said, and then there was a crackling burst of static as the Horizon entered the wormhole. Deathly silence filled the control room as all they could do was wait for the Horizon to emerge from the other side. There was a danger that the ship would be crushed by the pressures of the wormhole.

"How long is it supposed to take them to get to the other side?" one woman asked, worry etched upon her face.

"It depends on the wormhole, but we estimate that it should take them around five minutes to travel through this particular one," Sirius said.

"It already feels like hours," the woman said, laughing nervously. A few other people joined in. Sirius wondered what it would be like for the astronauts to travel through a wormhole. They were traversing vast distances in the blink of an eye and he was eager to find out what kind of effect it would have on the human mind. Images from probes had shown the inside of a wormhole to be an iridescent swirl of vivid colours, but there could only be so much gleaned from a computerised image. The human experience counted for far more than that and the crew of the Horizon were blessed to be experiencing something that no other human had.

The silence was broken by more crackling static through which Captain Chung's voice could be heard. There was a great cheer as the Horizon made it through the first wormhole and they were quickly silenced by Captain Chung's voice.

"...have just travelled through the wormhole. It was...it was beautiful, like flying threw a sea of jewels. We're fixing telemetry for the next wormhole and...my God...no it...it can't be..." Chung's voice faded. The people in the control room looked at each other worried and panicked.

"Please clarify, Horizon. What are you seeing? Is there something dangerous out there? Have you encountered alien life?"

There was a pregnant pause before Captain Chung replied. "No, Control, no. There are no aliens here. In fact, there's...there's *nothing*."

*

Sirius staggered into Matilda's house and slumped down, sighing and deflated.

"Well, I thought after last night you might be a little happier to see me," Matilda said, pouting playfully. Sirius groaned and couldn't even muster a smile. Matilda realized something was wrong and sat beside him, placing a hand on his shoulder.

"What happened today? I know technically you're not supposed to talk about it, but surely you can at least tell me if the mission was a success or not? I was expecting to hear something on the news, but aside from a vague statement-"

"There's nothing out there..." Sirius croaked. The words sounded hollow and he couldn't even believe that they were real.

"What do you mean by nothing? It's the universe. It can't just be empty," Matilda said with a laugh, but the laugh faded when Sirius looked at her with his wide, haunted eyes that were heavy with sorrow.

"There's nothing, Matilda. The Horizon made it through the first wormhole and saw nothing but dying stars and dead planets. They made a couple more trips, but the farther out they went, the less there was, until there was just... a void. They came back to Earth. They're all safe, but we're...we live in a dead universe, Matilda. There's nothing out there."

"Nothing? Like, no aliens or anything?"

"Nothing!" Sirius said sharply, startling Matilda. "If there were any aliens, they have all died out, probably a long time ago, possibly even before the human race was a twinkle in God's eye." He let out a scoffing laugh. "I think we were born too late. To think of all the life that had lived before us and we can't meet any of it."

From the expression on her face, Sirius could tell that Matilda was still trying to come to terms with it all. It was a feeling he understood well as it had been hours since he had been there in the control room when Horizon had sent through their report, and he still hadn't come to terms with it. His hands trembled and there was a queasy, churning feeling that hadn't settled in the pit of his stomach.

"But maybe that just means that life is going to spring up again, that we can give birth to a whole new universe!"

Sirius hated to be the one to dampen her enthusiasm, but he couldn't deny the truth he had heard.

"You don't understand, Matilda, there is no hope for new life. We live in a dying universe. It's surrounding us, coming for us, and there's nothing we can do to stop it. The universe has already died and we're just waiting for it to happen. All those images we saw of a thriving cosmos were echoes of the past. The only thing left is time."

Matilda remained silent as realization dawned on her face. In fact, she went through as many emotions as Sirius had experienced when he first heard the news. He remembered the hollow, despondent tone of the astronauts as they spoke of what they saw. Their voices were filled with terror, as though they were agents of doom, seers that had seen the end of the world.

"And they're keeping this a secret?"

Sirius nodded. "They thought it was best to not induce panic. They're going to discuss the matter with the world leaders first, but the likelihood is that they're going to come up with some story to prevent people from panicking."

"That's crazy! They can't keep this from people. We have to do something, Sirius!" Matilda cried. Sirius thought it sweet that she was so married to the truth. Sweet, but hopeless.

"No, we can't do anything. Can you imagine what's going to happen if people learn that we live in a dying universe? Can you imagine all the existential crises that are going to grip people? If people don't have a purpose, then they will be capable of anything. We always looked at the stars for hope, but it mocks us with its emptiness. The yearning to explore has united us and given us a purpose, something to strive for. Without that fire to keep us going, we'll descend into anarchy again. There are going to be more wars," Sirius' tone grew more despairing as he pictured the future of the human race. "People are going to realize that the only thing we have to conquer is this planet and nobody is ever going to be satisfied. Matilda, I developed the Endescope to give humanity a new frontier to explore, but instead I've only shown that we have no future."

Sirius had been wondering what he was going to do with his life, and now he realized there wasn't much point to anything. His entire accomplishment had only shown the grim truth. Humanity always needed something to strive towards; perhaps space was something that they should never have conquered. Perhaps it would have been better had they always lived in ignorance, if this had been one boundary that wouldn't be crossed.

"That's not true, Sirius. We still have a future. We still have each other."

"That's sweet of you to say and I don't mean any offence with this, but it all seems rather trivial given what we've learned, doesn't it?"

If Matilda was hurt by what he said, she did not show any sign of it. Instead, she shifted her position and took his hands. She gazed at him directly. "Sirius, you told me that the beauty of science and scientists is that it adapts to new information. It doesn't have any sentiment about what should be or what should happen, only what *is*. You looked in another direction to everyone else and you found hope. Maybe the same thing needs to happen now. You said that we've always been looking to the stars for inspiration and for our future, but maybe this just goes to show we've always been wrong. Maybe we should..." her voice caught on emotion for a moment, "maybe we should be looking at each other."

Sirius tilted his head up to look at her. She tilted her head and in her eyes he saw something shimmering and beautiful, as though all the colours of the world were dancing before him, creating something unique and vibrant. He had always looked to the stars, to the infinite horizon that awaited them, but when he looked into her eyes, he saw something else, something that filled him with the same wonder as he felt as a child. There was another horizon to chart, another place filled with mystery and awe, and it was one that wasn't dead yet – the human heart. Sirius didn't know how long it would take for a universe to die, but he was confident it would be long enough for a man to fall in love.

He looked down and saw Matilda's hand nestled in his palm. He breathed in her scent and then he tasted the sweetness of her lips. She rose and led him into the bedroom, and suddenly the rest of the universe didn't seem to matter.

The Suitcase

"We're not getting paid enough for this," Ian muttered as he and Charlie opened the door to the basement of the Esquire hotel. The building had stood in London for over a century. It was an historical sight and yet was not immune to the effects of social evolution. The old building was being renovated to become a boutique hotel. Situated in the heart of London, it was in a prime location, but before it was renovated, there was a lot of work that needed to be done to clear it out. Over the course of so many decades, a lot of things had been accumulated in the basement. Charlie and Ian were part of the crew hired to clean the hotel out, and they had been given the unenviable task of taking on the basement.

The basement was more like a vault, a huge chamber that was filled with boxes, old furniture, filing cabinets and a musty smell. Charlie sighed as he descended the metal stairs.

"Well, I guess we'd better get on with it...
Otherwise it's just going to take us longer,"
Charlie said. Ian rolled his eyes and shook
his head; the flesh around his jaws wobbled
like jelly. Ian's hair was wispy and white, his
frame was stocky and his hands were
gnarled after a lifetime of manual labour.
Charlie was a decade or so younger than him
and in Ian he saw his future. Already there
were grunts and aches that peppered his
body and hadn't been there before. Slowly
but surely, he had grown old. He wasn't
entirely sure at which point in his life the
change had taken place.

"You'd have thought they'd send some of
the younger lads down here. At our age, we
should be getting the easy jobs," Ian
grumbled, moving towards a stack of boxes.

"Well, they're all a sort of clique now,
aren't they? They have their fun on the
weekends. Guess we're not the kind of guys
they want joining them on a night out."

"Not that I can blame them. The last place I
want to be after a hard week's work is
standing in a night club with music blaring
in my head. I don't know how they do it."

"The joy of youth," Charlie offered Ian a grin, but it wasn't returned. Ian muttered under his breath as he started to lift boxes off of shelves and carry them back towards the stairs. Once they had piled up enough, they would take it out to a huge skip and it would in turn be taken to the dump.

"It's a real pity that this place is being renovated. I remember hearing about this place when I was younger. It was the place to be, you know? You'd made it if you stayed at the Esquire. I used to think that one day I'd stay here as well," Ian said with a dry chuckle.

"Well, you could probably squat in one of the rooms now if you wanted. I doubt anyone is going to check until they start stripping the walls."

"It makes you sick, doesn't it, seeing things being torn down, making way for the new."

"It's just the way of the world. It keeps on turning no matter what."

"Yeah, and before you know it, your life has flashed before your eyes and everything has just gone..." Ian's voice trailed away. Charlie pressed his lips together and stared at his colleague. Ian wasn't exactly a friend, although Charlie saw him more often than most of his friends, especially nowadays when they were all so busy with their families they barely had time to meet. Charlie took a break from sorting out the boxes and ran a hand through his light blonde hair. As he did so, a sleeve rolled up, revealing a tattoo.

"How are you coping, Ian? You must miss her a lot."

Ian stood with his back facing Charlie. "You have no idea. You're lucky, Charlie. I hope you make sure you appreciate your woman every day."

"I do," Charlie said, although he ignored the thought that told him he was lying.

"One minute she's there, annoying you no end, the next she's gone and there's nothing you can do," his voice trailed away. Charlie wished that he knew what to say or what to do. He'd never been very good at things like this, especially not with a man like Ian, a man who he'd known for years, but only through work. They had spent a lot of time together, but there was still a sense of a barrier between them. In a way, they were warhorses too; the crew they worked with was getting younger and younger as people retired, moved on and were replaced by others. Recently, it had begun to feel that the world was shifting and changing while he stayed in one place.

"I guess all you can do is remember her. People aren't really gone as long as you remember them," Charlie offered. He had heard people saying that, although he wasn't sure if it actually helped any. Ian shrugged and sighed, and then he continued with his job.

"I never thought I'd end up clearing out a hotel basement," Ian said after some time, taking a break where he mopped sweat off his brow and sat on a box. He puffed out his reddened cheeks and hunched forward, looking as though he bore the weight of the world on his shoulders. "Life never works out the way you want it, does it? You know, I look at those kids up there and I pity them. I know they laugh at me and call me the old fool, but one day they're going to feel the same way I am. They think this is just a job, just a bit of cash on the side before their life starts in earnest, but it never does. They're going to be the same as you and me, Charlie, mark my words."

Charlie continued to gather boxes and stack them near the stairs. He thought on Ian's words and felt a stone of sorrow in his stomach. Life certainly hadn't turned out the way he'd thought. When he was younger, he assumed that one day everything would make sense, that one day he would be able to live without fearing about what might happen in the future or what might happen to his family.

"We're not that bad," Charlie said, trying to fight against the despair that was in his mind. He had never given too much thought to the meaning of life or the grand purpose of cosmic energy. He'd never had the intellectual capacity to do that, but over recent years, there had been a general unsettling feeling of unease creeping in his mind; at this point, he wasn't sure if it would ever go away.

"Well, I suppose you're alright, given that you have a kid. That's all we really live for anyway, isn't it? Without the future generation, there's nothing there. It's about this time that I regret not having kids. Before Marie died, I never thought much of it. I know it's the done thing and people always looked at us strangely for never having kids, but the truth is that we only ever needed each other. But that was short-sighted. When she was gone, well, I wish I had someone around. At least you didn't make the same mistake. How is Jess anyway?"

Charlie arched his eyebrows as he thought about Jess. "Getting older all the time," he said. "Wilder too." There was a time when she doted on her father, but now she seemed to see him as the enemy. It was the natural order of things, especially with teenagers, Charlie supposed, but it still didn't make it any easier.

"Well, at least you won't be alone in your old age," Ian said. Charlie nodded and resumed work. He got the sense that Ian was reaching out to him, trying to find some sort of connection that would end the loneliness, but it wouldn't quite take. And Charlie didn't know how to handle that anyway. He gave enough of himself to his family that he wasn't sure if he had anything to give to someone else.

Ian wheezed as he lurched back into the basement. It was really a job for more than two men, but the rest of the guys were going to slack off and do what they wanted anyway. It was how things had gone since the old guys had gone. Ian and Charlie were the two remnants left, and Charlie feared that things were only going to get worse. It was just a shame that there wasn't a way out. Given his age and the economy, there was nothing he could do about the path he was on. The world didn't like people changing their paths in life. You had to choose something when you were young and hope that it would serve you well. Nowadays, it seemed more often than not that people drifted into despair and ended up wishing that things could be different with no way to change things.

It was a bleak day and, in truth, it was a bleak job. Usually when they stripped a building, it was an old house where the foundations had rotted and needed replacing. Rarely was there a sense of history behind it. Rarely did he tread in a place that had housed dreams. As he rummaged through shelves, he came across old booklets and programmes of celebrities and showmen, as sepia toned as the memories of those who had actually seen these performances. There were photographs as well, showing people in glamorous outfits, all wearing smiles on their faces. It was a world of glitz and glamour that he could have never experienced for himself. No doubt in those halcyon days of the past they never would have imagined that the Esquire would be torn down and repackaged, this time not a haven for the famous, but a refuge for those who could afford it. Charlie had overheard how much the rooms were going to cost and it boggled his mind how anyone could afford to spend so much on something so frivolous. It proved to him, as if it needed to be proven, that society was split and there was no way to ascend to the upper echelons.

The entire history of the hotel was held in this basement and it was all going to be forgotten, cast aside as though it held no inherent worth. Was that all their lives amounted to? Part of Charlie wished that he could take some of this back, to preserve the past, but he didn't have room at home and Vicky wouldn't appreciate him bringing back some old tat. With a heavy sigh, he carried more things out to the skip and then returned, ignoring the laughter of the other men who were sitting around, enjoying one of their frequent breaks.

It was a short while later that Charlie found something that caught his attention. He had pulled away a number of boxes and then revealed a suitcase. It was made of dark leather and it had crinkles and lines that suggested it had been used a lot, and yet it was consigned here. There were initials on the suitcase – E.L. – along with a lock. He ran his hands along the surface and sensed something else, some kind of energy that radiated out from the suitcase. It was almost as though it called to him. He picked it up and carried it to the stairs, placing it beside a few other boxes.

As he got back to work, he kept glancing over at the suitcase. He wasn't sure why it fascinated him so, but he couldn't take his mind off it. When Ian was ready to take some things out to the skip, Charlie called out to him and told him that he would take care of the suitcase. Ian shrugged and carried on, while Charlie wondered why he felt this strongly about the suitcase. He wasn't usually taken with things he found at work. While it was against the code of conduct, he doubted that anyone would protest strongly against him taking something from the site, as long as it was just one thing. Since it had been in the basement of this hotel for decades at least, perhaps even a century, it wasn't as though the owner was going to come and beg for its return either.

When it came to the end of the day, Charlie picked up the suitcase and carried it back home. Nobody raised an eyebrow, although Charlie did breathe a sigh of relief when he left the site and nobody questioned him. There was just one thing that piqued his curiosity though; when he picked the suitcase up the second time, he was certain that it was a little heavier than when he had first found it.

*

Charlie returned home to the smell of bacon and eggs being cooked. The kitchen was filled with smoke. Vicky was on the phone with her mother. She gave Charlie a quick kiss when he entered and resumed her conversation without taking a breath. Charlie went out to the shed, which had become his little hobby home, and placed the suitcase on his table, pushing aside a model plane he had been working on. He examined the case again and tried to open it, although the lock seemed sturdy. Since it had been left in the hotel, it was probably the case that it was empty or that the contents inside were inconsequential. However, there was also the possibility that there was something valuable inside or something that might lead to an adventure. When he was younger, people had always told him that he was a dreamer and they had always admonished Charlie for this quality, so while he had suppressed it over the years, it hadn't entirely gone away.

The more he examined the suitcase, the more he became intimately aware of the wrinkles across the leather. He gazed at the initials, which were embossed in gold. Who was this E.L. and why had they left their suitcase in the hotel? The situation only became more curious when Charlie realized that the leather was peeling away from one corner. Charlie took it in his hand and pulled. There was a ripping sound as the leather peeled away and, as he peered under the flap, Charlie's brow furrowed. Breath rushed between his lips. He got a crafting knife and slid it along the leather, slicing away a whole line. When he pulled it away, he was faced with something that didn't make sense. Lights blinked and flashed underneath, but it seemed incongruous. The suitcase looked old, far older than this technology should have been married with, and he became worried that it might be some unexploded bomb.

Before he could examine it further, he was called back in for dinner.

Just as he walked into the kitchen, he heard the stomping footsteps of Jess coming down the stairs. Jess had taken strongly after her mother. Both of them were short, slender, with narrow noses and long, tawny brown hair. They also had a temper to match and there had been many points over the years when Charlie had longed for a son to even out the biological imbalance that existed within the house. Jess was fifteen and on the cusp of leaving school. When Charlie thought of her, he thought of the bubbly, happy girl she had been throughout her childhood. But that person had been replaced with a sullen, moody teenager that barely had two words to say to him. Vicky had grown distant as well, preferring to spend more time with her shows and speaking about those shows to her mother than with Charlie. There had been a time, long ago, when they had spent time together and enjoyed life together, but those memories were distant ones and it seemed as though they had been in a rut for a long time now. Not that either of them wanted anything to change; they were both far too scared to talk about their problems. He assumed that most people felt the same way, that life was something to be endured rather than enjoyed.

"Have you given any more thought to what you're going to do after school?" Charlie asked.

Jess rolled her eyes. "Oh, for God's sake, Dad, I don't need every meal to be an interrogation. I'm sure something will sort itself out."

Charlie bit his tongue and breathed heavily, hating that every time he brought up a sensitive topic with Jess she bit his head off. "I'm not trying to make you angry, Jess. I'm just trying to make you understand that you have to start making decisions because that's what life demands of you. If you don't know what you're going to do, that's fine, but I'm worried that you're not giving it enough thought and you're going to end up drifting aimlessly through life. I do wish that things could be different – believe me, I do – but I know that you've got a lot of talent and you could do some wonderful things. Are you still drawing?"

"On and off," Jess said bluntly between mouthfuls of bacon and eggs.

"Well, you should keep it up. You could really be a good artist."

"I don't know. There are lots of better people in the world than me."

"Just because you're not the best at something doesn't mean you can't make a living from it. I just don't want you to fall into a job like I did and then be defined by that for the rest of your life," Charlie hoped that Jess listened to his explanation and realized that it came from a heartfelt place. But recently he wasn't sure how she interpreted his words. Sometimes he said things that were sincere that made her explode with anger; a conversation with her was like walking through a minefield.

"You shouldn't sell yourself short, love," Vicky reached over and placed a hand on his arm. "There's nothing wrong with doing a good, honest day's work."

"I'm not saying there is... I'm just saying that she should look for opportunities while she has them available to her. You and I both know that life can move all too quickly and, before too long, you have more regrets than hopes."

His words silenced Vicky. Jess mumbled something and let her head drop, breaking eye contact with her father. It always seemed difficult to have an honest conversation with them. Sometimes Charlie wondered if he had a connection with them at all, for he found it difficult to know what was going on in their minds.

As soon as dinner was finished, Jess raced upstairs while Vicky moved to the front room, sinking in front of the TV. As Charlie washed up, he could hear Vicky begin to converse with her mother and he knew that the evening would be just the same as all the evenings before. He sighed as he dried his soapy hands and called to Vicky, saying that he would be out in the shed. He didn't hear her reply.

*

Charlie settled back into his seat and examined the suitcase again. This time, when he lifted it, it seemed heavier still, and he knew that it wasn't just a trick of the mind. Whatever was in the suitcase was growing and he started to wonder if he should have taken it at all. He lifted up the broken leather and looked at the blinking lights. It looked similar to modern technology, or perhaps even a little more advanced, but that shouldn't have been possible. He tried pressing the lights and the buttons, but nothing happened, so he did what any intrepid person would have done and took a screwdriver to it. If Charlie had been wiser, he might well have left it alone and not toyed around with things that he didn't understand, but Charlie had never claimed to be wise. Once he was interested in something, it was rare that anyone could dissuade him from following it to its natural end.

He fiddled about and managed to jimmy the suitcase open. The top popped off and Charlie grinned. He carefully lifted the lid of the suitcase, curious about what he was going to find. What waited for him was black, viscous ooze. It was a pool of shadows, shimmering as the faint light danced upon it. The ooze was odourless and it moved around the suitcase as though it was a lake. Charlie frowned. He hadn't seen anything like this before. It looked almost like oil, but it didn't smell anything like it. He leaned down so that he could peer in closer, to the point where his nose was level with the edge of the suitcase. It was on an even surface, but even so the ooze shifted and moved, as though it was alive.

A lump formed in his throat and fear crawled over his skin. Why would anyone have left this in a suitcase? What even was it? The more he gazed into the ooze, the more it transfixed him. For brief moments, there seemed to be flickers and flashes of images, but they were gone before he could fully understand what they were. There was still something that drew him towards the ooze, something that compelled him and enchanted him. He reached out with his hand and touched the ooze with the tip of his finger. It was oddly cold. He brought his hand back, seeking to inspect his fingertip, but as he did so, he pulled the ooze back with him in a long, dark line. No matter how much he pulled, the ooze wouldn't break free. Panic flared within him as he took his other hand and tried to peel the ooze away, but this just led it to covering his other palm.

And then Charlie realized it was beginning to spread. He wasn't just being pulled towards the ooze in a metaphorical sense, but in a very real sense. The ooze was exerting force, guiding him towards the suitcase. The cold darkness spread over his hands and wrists, extending up his forearms. The ooze widened and expanded as it pulled him down like quicksand. Charlie struggled and writhed, fighting against the black ooze, but it was hopeless. His eyes widened as the darkness engulfed him and, just as he was about to scream, it covered his mouth, suffocating him, the coldness running over his tongue and down his throat. He gagged and shuddered as he was swallowed by the ooze, scared out of his mind because he didn't know what this was or why it had claimed him. Perhaps he was just the wrong man at the wrong time. Perhaps he should have been smarter and left the suitcase where it belonged. He was submerged in the ooze and his last thoughts were of his wife and his daughter, and how much he wished his life had been different.

*

Charlie hadn't expected to experience anything else. Once the ooze had claimed him, he assumed that he would be dead, so when he awoke in what could only be described as another realm, he was unsettled. A chill crept around him and even though he pulled his clothes more tightly around him and rubbed his arms, it didn't have any effect. He looked down and saw that he was standing on black, slick ground. He lifted his feet tentatively and was grateful to see that the ooze was not attached to his feet. Whatever it was, it had swallowed him, and now he was inside it. It was as though he was in a huge black igloo. There was space for him to move, but the boundaries of the world were clearly defined in a dome that rose all around him. It had the same shimmering quality that he had seen in the suitcase.

"H...Hello," he said in a small, frightened voice. His word drifted into silence. There was nothing there to respond to him. He took a few steps to the side and wondered again what this thing was. Just as he thought this, a shape began to form before him. He staggered back as the black ooze formed an eldritch monstrosity that rose from a dark pit. It writhed, its tendrils reaching high above it. Whether it was reaching for mercy or with threat Charlie could not tell, but he recoiled in horror and turned his face away, lifting his hands to give himself even more protection. His thoughts turned to home and the people he had left behind. When he was brave enough to open his eyes again he saw that the ooze had reshaped itself, this time becoming silhouettes of Vicky and Jess. A smile formed on his face at their images, and then he realized that the ooze was taking prompts from his thoughts.

To test his hypothesis, he focused his mind on something else. The first thing that came to him was the model plane he had been working on. Almost immediately the ooze reshaped and grew, becoming first a representation of the model plane, and then growing bigger, becoming the size of the actual fighter jet, looming before him in a sleek form of darkness and shadow. The wings jutted out, the nose pointed forward, the shape was imbued with power and a smile formed on his face. He reached out and touched the plane; it was still cold, but it felt *real*.

Turning, he thought of other things. A lion rose and majestically strode along a prairie, before it was replaced with a wrecking ball that swung through the air like a pendulum. Then, a football stadium appeared. He kept it tiny so that he towered above it like a god looking down from the heavens. The ooze had made 22 tiny little players, each one distinct even though they were all made from the same substance. He was enthralled by the rhythm of the game before he thought of something else and the image dispersed, splashing away into nothingness. In one moment, something vibrant had been captured and then it was dismissed just as easily. The ooze rose and a look of wonder appeared on his face as a monstrous T-Rex formed before him, based on his memory of the skeleton found in the Natural History Museum. The black bones looked horrific and the hollow eyes filled him with fear. The jagged teeth were swirling and sharp, and the huge bulk of its body twisted from side to side as it lurched forward. Charlie watched it stalk for prey, before it too disappeared and returned to the ooze.

He stayed there for a long time. It was as though this was a place where his imagination could come to life and anything could be formed. He had a feeling he had only just tapped the full potential of it as well. The more he practised, the better he got at holding two distinct thoughts at the same time and getting things to interact. He was only limited by his own imagination and it was at this point he wished he was more creative.

Eventually, Charlie began to think of home again. An image of the building rose beside him, but it wasn't the same. The novelty of this place was astounding, but it wasn't home and he wasn't sure how to get back. But just as he thought of this, there was the same sensation he had experienced when he was pulled into the ooze. He could feel his body being guided away, being controlled by a force that was not his own. The ooze rose up his ankles and legs this time rather than his wrists and arms. Charlie was rooted in place as he braced himself for the same suffocating feeling that had engulfed him before. The cold ooze wrapped him in a cloak of darkness, embracing him in its eldritch, alien grip, and there was nothing he could do about it.

*

Charlie gasped as he pulled himself out of the suitcase, managing to free himself from the ooze, or perhaps it was that the ooze freed itself from him. He turned around and immediately slammed the suitcase shut, forcing it to lock again. None of the ooze had slipped out and he was glad for this. He breathed heavily as he tried to process what he had seen. He felt all around his body to make sure that everything was where it should be. He then looked at the model plane he had been working on. It was exactly the same as the image that had been pulled from his mind. He wasn't yet sure what this meant or what the implications were. Who was he even supposed to tell about this thing?

He staggered up to his bedroom. He cleaned his teeth in a trance. Vicky and Jess had already gone to sleep. He'd been in the ooze far longer than he had realized. He groaned as he sank into bed and pulled the covers over him, glad for a sense of respite, annoyed that he had stayed up too late, which meant that he was going to feel as rough as hell the following day.

"Charlie, are you okay?" Vicky asked gently, her voice as soft as velvet in the small hours of the night.

"Yeah, I'm fine. Just lost track of time, love," he said, leaning over to peck her on the forehead. That was about all the intimacy they had nowadays, not that Charlie minded much. The world had ground him down to such an extent that he couldn't summon the thrill of excitement within him any longer. "What are you doing up anyway?"

"I couldn't sleep. I've had a lot on my mind lately."

"Oh, yeah?" he said, half-interested as he really wanted to sleep, but he knew what the price was for ignoring Vicky when she wanted to talk.

"I was thinking about something you said earlier, about living with more regrets than hopes. Is that how you really feel? Do you regret your life... our life?"

"No, of course not, I mean...it's just that I regret that things turned out this way. I always wanted to do something important with my life, you know? I thought that one day we wouldn't have to struggle for money or wonder what we're going to do next. I thought that, at some point, our lives would be filled with adventure, but instead we just do the same thing day in and day out. It's not a judgment on you or anything, it's just the way the world is, I suppose. Everything keeps getting more expensive. It always seems as though the past was better."

"Yeah, I guess I know how you feel. I think that's why I've been so obsessed with TV lately. I just want to escape to another world. I wish things could be better. I worry for Jess as well. I try to be on her side and to support her, but I share the same concerns as you do. I don't know what she's going to do with her life and now it seems that if you don't make a decision quickly you miss your chance. I'm not sure she quite realizes how difficult it is out there."

"No, and she's not going to take our word for it either," Charlie said dryly. He thought about telling Vicky about this wondrous thing he had discovered, but he wasn't sure where to begin, so he kept it to himself for now.

"It will be okay, won't it, Charlie?"

"Of course it will," Charlie took Vicky in his arms and kissed her on the cheek. They held each other in their small house, finding comfort in each other while the despair of the world swirled outside, ready to make victims of them all.

*

"You look like hell, Charlie. Did you have a late one last night? Don't tell me you went out with them. You know men our age can't cope with that," Ian said scolding him. Charlie rubbed the dark shadows under his eyes and shook his head. Frankly, it had been tempting to not come into work at all once he woke up with a splitting headache. All he'd wanted to do was return to the ooze and play around in the space of possibility.

"Just had a late night talking with the wife," Charlie said. Ian's lips thinned as he nodded. They went back down to the basement to resume their duties. Charlie wondered if there was anything else hiding in the basement that was going to surprise him. He rummaged around various boxes and tried to find more information about the history of the hotel, but it seemed as though the records only went back so far. He was looking for any record of anyone with a name beginning with the initials 'E.L.', but he couldn't find any. He couldn't even see who had first built and managed the hotel either.

As he reflected on his experience in the ooze, he thought about the first thing he had seen. He had asked himself what the ooze was and where it had come from. In response, the ooze had formed the image of a tentacle creature. Was it possible that the ooze was alive and was capable of communicating with him? Charlie was sure that he hadn't formed the tentacle image out of his own mind. The thought that he shared a space with some kind of entity was eerie and made him shudder, yet he was still tempted to go back inside.

He didn't find anything like the suitcase in the basement and the day largely passed without incident. Charlie was anxious for the day to end because he wanted to return home and also because he was slightly worried about having left the suitcase in the shed. If the ooze was alive, then would the suitcase be able to keep it from escaping? Had he clamped it shut strongly enough? Vicky and Jess knew well enough to stay out of his shed, but what if by chance they had gone in and found the ooze themselves? There were too many questions, too many unknowns for his liking and the tension coiled within him, nestling in the pit of his stomach.

It was in the middle of the afternoon when there was some commotion upstairs. Charlie and Ian glanced at each other before they rose and went to see what was going on. They emerged from the basement to see the foremen and the other guys trying to ward off an old man. He was creaking and wheezing, looking almost a hundred years old. His back was hunched and he trembled.

"Let me down there! I need to see it!" he cried out in his reedy, wheezing voice.

"You don't need to see anything, old man. This is a building site. We can't just have anyone wandering in. Get out of here for your own safety," the foreman said gruffly.

Three of them approached the old man, appearing more threatening than they needed to.

"My name is Eddie Leonard and you have to let me in!"

As soon as the old man spoke his name, something twigged in Charlie's mind. He raced out and told the others that he would escort the man out. They grunted at his appearance. The foreman told him not to take too much time else it would be taken out of his pay.

"No, you can't make me leave. Please. I need to get down to the basement," the old man said, his voice plaintive and thin. Charlie took hold of his arm and turned him around.

"It's okay. I think I know what you're looking for. We need to talk," Charlie said. They walked outside and made their way down an alley. Cars rushed by, noise exploding around them, but Charlie didn't care much for that. He looked at the old man, who still had a desperate look in his eyes.

"Are you looking for the suitcase?"

"The suitcase... yes..." he said, a wave of relief passing over him. "Is it there? Please, you must tell me it's still there."

"It's...it's safe," Charlie said.

Eddie peered at him and narrowed his eyes. They were milky, yet intense.

"You...you took it, didn't you? You've seen it."

Charlie's gaze darted away. He cleared his throat and shifted his feet. "I didn't mean to take it. I just... Something came over me. What the hell is it?"

A thin smile appeared on Eddie's lips and he nodded his head. "Good, good... It still knows how to speak. It called me once too," he said.

"Who are you and what is it?"

"Take me to it," Eddie said. His voice had a surprising amount of strength considering how old he was. Charlie got the sense that if he wanted any answers, he was going to have to do as Eddie asked. He thought about the warning from the foreman, but decided that learning more about this suitcase and the ooze held inside was worth the risk. He took Eddie home, sneaking around the back to the shed, only to find that the case was open. The ooze was a slick pool.

"I thought I closed it," Charlie said.

"You fool. You shouldn't leave this open!" Eddie cried.

Charlie's heart was in his mouth as he thought about Vicky and Jess. Had one of them been swallowed?

"I've brought you here. You need to tell me what this thing is," Charlie said urgently, standing in between Eddie and the door, not that Eddie was spry enough to get away from Charlie.

Eddie breathed heavily. He reached out and placed his hand near the suitcase, although he did not touch the ooze. "I was the guardian for a long time. I thought it would be safe in the hotel. Then, I saw people inside. I saw the works and I thought that the suitcase was not safe any longer. I should have found another way."

"Another way to do what?"

"To stop the unthinkable from happening. This thing is nameless. It is not from our world, but it is connected to others. The Esquire is built on a cosmic hub of sorts, a place where different dimensions intersect, where thought and time and reality are merged. This suitcase, this ooze is the lock that prevents anything else from coming through. There has been a pact through time, through generations. We watch over the ooze and the ooze watches over us, stops anything from coming through. We cannot take it away from the hotel. You must find a way to take it back. There must always be a guardian. I...I cannot do it any longer, so you must find a way to get it back to the hotel."

"But the whole place is being cleared. I don't know where I can hide it so that it would be safe."

"Then you must find somewhen else."

"Did you say some*when*?"

A smile cracked on Eddie's face. "You still don't know what it's fully capable of, do you? This ooze is a gateway. It can link you with the past. You could take the suitcase back, hide it in a better place than I could, somewhere deeper than the basement. Then you could return here. Yes, that is the only way."

"And what happens if I don't?"

"The end of the world," Eddie said gravely. "Huge, monstrous things that only want to consume. They'll rip this world apart until there's nothing left. There are already dying stars out there, stars that have been dimmed by the darkness."

"And this ooze is the only thing holding it back"? Charlie said with disbelief.

Before Eddie could answer, the ooze shifted and churned and then a form emerged. Jess stood before them, a look of shock and disbelief etched upon her face. She turned to Charlie and gave him a huge grin.

"Dad, what the hell is this? It's amazing!" she yelled, transfixed by the ooze.

"Apparently it's the only thing that's standing between us and the rest of the universe," Charlie said.

*

"Okay, so what you're telling me is that you took a suitcase from the hotel. In this suitcase is some weird alien entity that acts as a portal between reality and time, and it's in our shed right now, but you need to take it back because if it's not in the Esquire hotel, alien creatures are going to come and destroy the planet?" Vicky asked, a look of disbelief upon her face.

Charlie, Eddie and Jess all looked at each other.

"That's about it," Charlie said.

"The hotel is sat upon a nexus point," Eddie explained, but he couldn't get anything else out because Jess spoke enthusiastically.

"You have to see it, Mom, it's amazing. The things you can do in there and the things you can see... It's just... It's crazy. It was as though the whole world opened up to me. I saw so many things! So many places..."

"Places?" Charlie frowned. "When I was inside, I could only see things from my own mind."

"Oh, no, Dad, it's much more than that," Jess said excitedly. "It was as though I saw so much history. I was able to see what happened, what Eddie is talking about. The ooze showed me these things attacking different worlds, covering them in shadow. The ooze is from a dying race that sacrificed themselves to save as many other worlds as they could. They spread themselves over the cosmos to protect us."

"I think I'm going to need a drink. What does any of this means?" Vicky said.

"Well, Eddie seems to think that we need to put the suitcase back into the hotel," Charlie said.

"But if this ooze is so powerful, why does it need to be kept in this suitcase anyway?" Vicky asked. All eyes turned to Eddie.

"Because the ooze will always expand if it is not held within the suitcase. The suitcase has technology from the ooze's home planet that helps it maintain its vigil over us. There is something about our atmosphere that causes it to lose cohesion if it is not properly guarded."

"Okay, so what is the plan now?" Vicky asked.

"I think Eddie is suggesting that I take this suitcase back in time, hide it in the hotel somewhere deeper than the basement so that it won't be discovered," Charlie said.

"You want to travel back in time?" Vicky blinked and spoke with scepticism in her voice. "Am I the only one who is having a really hard time following this?" she asked.

"You have to free your mind from the trappings of time," Eddie said. He fetched a number of items from the kitchen and was about to launch into an elaborate explanation of time travel and how the rules could be bent from different perspectives when there was a knock at the door.

"Who on earth could that be?" Vicky said, exasperated. Charlie rose from the kitchen table to open the door. When he stood there, he saw a woman who looked the spitting image of Jess and Vicky. She was dressed in an elegant pink dress and wore sparkling earrings. Her skin was tanned and her hair was thick and lustrous. She wore a wide smile and clasped her hands in front of her stomach, as though she had to stop herself from lunging forward.

"Can I help you?" Charlie asked.

"Actually, I might be able to help *you*, as long as I have the right day. Do you have the suitcase? And is Eddie here?"

Charlie stared at her blankly and then sighed, choosing to give up rather than understand anything. He shook his head and stepped aside, pointing to the kitchen. The woman walked into the house and looked around, marvelling as though she was in a museum. When she walked into the kitchen, she saw Jess and her hands rose to her mouth. Tears welled in her eyes and she was unable to stop herself from flinging her arms around Jess. Jess frowned.

"Who the hell are you?" she asked.

"I'm Emily, your granddaughter," she said.

*

"Okay, I'm definitely getting this drink. This is too weird," Vicky said, grabbing some wine from the cupboard and pouring herself a tall glass. "Who the hell are you and what are you doing here?"

Charlie had joined them in the kitchen and listened with interest. Emily was well-spoken and seemed to have done very well for herself. If she was his great-granddaughter, then he could be proud.

"I was told that you'd all find this difficult to believe. Please, be patient. Basically, I was sent here to make sure that certain events unfold in the way they have to. I'm actually buying the Esquire hotel."

"*You?*" Vicky said in one breath.

"Yes, at the insistence of my family. It's been our mission to ensure that it stays on site, to protect the ooze, to protect the entire world," she said.

"What a minute, you're from the past?" Vicky asked.

"Well, no, I'm from the present. I've been living here just the same as you have and I have to say that it's been a challenge not to meet you all, especially you, grandma," she turned to Jess, who leaned back and shook her head.

"I'm not sure I like being called that. How do we know you're on the level?" Jess asked.

Emily laughed a little. "I don't think anyone could come up with a story like this, but if you must ask, well..." she reached into her handbag and pulled out a small book. Charlie knew it to be Jess's. It was something he had gotten her for Christmas the previous year, although in Emily's hand it looked more worn and faded. She placed it on the table and slid it over towards Jess. Jess took it and looked at it with disbelief.

"No, this…this can't be," she said as she flicked through the pages. Charlie craned over her shoulder as she moved from the back of the sketchbook to the front. She threw it down on the table and rushed upstairs. Within moments, she returned with a sketchbook that looked in much better form. She opened both of them at the same time. The initial drawings were the same, but where there were blank pages in the book she owned, there were vibrant and vivid drawings in the book that Emily had given her.

"This is…this is unreal." Jess said. Vicky and Charlie crowded around her to examine it for themselves.

"This is proof," Emily said, smiling gently. "I know that it's difficult for you to believe, but you wanted me to come back here to make sure that you went back in time, to convince you that you did what needed to be done."

"What do you mean? I told you to come here?" Jess said, looking up from the sketchbook.

Emily nodded and smiled. "When I was younger, you used to tell me that one day I would do something very special. You talked about your family and your old life, how unhappy you all were in this place. You told me how scared you were about the future and that you didn't think you would find a place in the world, and how you really wanted to tell your father that, but you were ashamed. When you had the opportunity, you all decided to go back in time with the ooze and live in the past, becoming the managers of the Esquire hotel. You made wise investments and became a part of the elite, making sure that your descendants had a strong foundation for life, and to make sure that there would always be someone there to protect the ooze. You started a property company with the intention of buying the Esquire outright as soon as it went on the market, a company that I now manage. I'm going to ensure that the ooze stays safe, but you have to do the same. You have to go back in time."

Vicky, Charlie, and Jess all gazed at each other.

"Jess, is this true? Are you really scared?"

Jess looked down at her sketchbooks and nodded. "I didn't know how to tell you. There are so few opportunities for people my age. I know you want the best for me. I just didn't know how I was going to go about it. I thought that I was going to get lost in the cracks."

"Now you don't have to. You're a great artist," Emily smiled and gestured to the sketchbooks.

"But I haven't... I can't do this," Jess flicked through the paintings.

"You will," Emily said. "Please, it all relies on you going back into the past."

"I'm still not sure about this. I haven't even been into the ooze and all of this time travel stuff doesn't make any sense to me. How can there be two suitcases at the same time and, if there's a chance of us not going back, then why are you even here? I'm not sure I like the idea that my great-granddaughter is telling me what I have to do with my life," Vicky said bitterly. Charlie put his hand on her shoulder trying to reassure her.

"It's still your decision, just as it was your decision to tell Jess to tell me that I have to come here and talk with you. It's a just a decision you haven't made yet. In a sense, it's a decision that you're always going to make. You just don't know it yet."

Vicky shook her head and there was still a look of disbelief on her face. Jess flicked through the sketchbook and then wore a look of stern determination.

"We have to do this, Mum. Dad, you know what it's like in the ooze. It's important. If this stuff is true, then we have to go back. We can't risk it. And think of what it means for us. Come on, we're not going anywhere here. Our lives are at a dead end. This is what we've been waiting for. I've seen the way you look at each other, the way you ghost through life. Is this what you really want, for us to be on autopilot? Dad, I know you hate your job. I hear the way you grunt and groan all the time. How much longer do you think you're going to be able to do this? We're just getting unhappier with every day that passes. If there's a better future for us in the past, then I want to seize it for myself. Mum, I promise, once you see what the ooze can do, you'll understand, I swear."

Vicky still looked conflicted, but Charlie wasn't.

"She's right. We can't go on like this. If we're given this opportunity, we have to take it. How many times have we thought to ourselves that things could be better if only we had a chance to make it better? This is our chance, Vicky. We have a chance to do it all again and I've seen the pictures in the hotel. There was a party every night. We finally have a chance to live the life we've always dreamed of, a life where we don't have to feel like we're imprisoned by circumstances. I don't want to live out my days always wondering what might have been. I want to die knowing that I've lived life to the fullest; that's not going to happen if we stay here. It's not our fault – it's just the way the world is – but we're lucky enough to have been given the opportunity to escape. We have to take it."

Vicky breathed slowly, but eventually she nodded. She reached up and placed her hand on Charlie's. He felt the warmth of her skin and enjoyed the comfortable familiarity of it. He looked to Emily and smiled. "I'm sorry that we didn't get the chance to know each other better. It would have been nice to spend some time with you."

"It's okay. Grandma told me lots of stories about you. I've been with you all my life," Emily said. Then she turned to Eddie. "I'm sorry that I couldn't come and find you before this. I wanted to make sure that I didn't do anything to contaminate time, but I can look after you now."

"I understand, child," Eddie said.

"Emily, one more thing. There's a man I work with – Ian. Could you find some job for him so that he can be a little more comfortable? He's had a rough life and he's lost a lot. He could use a break."

"I'll make sure of it," Emily said. Charlie was filled with a warm feeling. It brought him great joy to know that one day his family would continue and serve a noble cause. He hadn't realized until that moment how much it had truly meant to him. They hugged Emily and refrained from asking her too many things about their future and her past. All Emily said was that they would be happy and that was enough for them.

Eddie then explained how it was going to work. Once inside the ooze, all they had to do was think about a certain place in time and a gateway would open up and they would pass through a time stream. The family made their way to the shed and held hands as they opened up the suitcase. Charlie smiled at his wife and daughter as they reached in and let the ooze seep over them, pulling them into its world.

*

Vicky gasped as she checked herself once they were in the ooze. Charlie looked around in wonder as Jess danced around and showed Vicky what the ooze was capable of. She could imagine things that were beyond his understanding. Instead of mere objects, she managed to give life to feelings and ideas, to music and different concepts. Instead of just creating shapes, she was creating a whole world that was budding and vibrant with life. A tear filled Charlie's eyes as he saw what she was capable of and, in that moment, it didn't matter as much that they were doing this to protect the world; if it gave his daughter the best chance of having a good life, then it was the right decision.

"I'm still not sure about this..." Vicky said.

"Mum, just look at what will happen if we don't," Jess said, pointing far away. The ooze coalesced into different spherical shapes. They were planets. From beyond came dark, jagged shards that slammed into the planets and fractured them. It was as violent a scene as any Charlie had witnessed. Vicky gasped. The destruction was on a scale that was almost incomprehensible to a human mind, but she started to nod as she realized that this was what they needed to do.

"It's going to be okay," Charlie said as he wrapped his arms around her. "It's all going to be okay, as long as we're together. That's the most important thing." He beckoned Jess towards him and they stood together as a family. They thought of the past and a portal appeared above them. The ooze wrapped around them in a cold, yet comforting embrace. It lifted them up above the world that Jess had created and an opening yawned before them. Around the edge images flickered like a film roll, images of people in elegant dresses and smart tuxedos sharing refined conversation and good times. Charlie knew he was finally going to be able to give his family the life they deserved. Relief washed over him and tension slipped away from his body. He finally felt free of the stresses of the modern world and how imprisoned he had felt by life. He looked upon his future with wide eyes, convinced that it had to be better than what came before. For the first time in a long time, he felt hope in his heart and looked forward to all the possibilities that would be presented to him.

The past was his future and, although from a certain point of view his life had already been lived, he was yet to live it. He held his family close to him as they passed through the portal to another time, a better time, where he could start anew.

Ahmu

Update protocol engaged.
AHMU unit downloading...
...

...
Update downloaded
Primary function maintained
All systems functional
Environmental controls secure
Security controls active
Area purified of toxins
Cleansing burst initiated
...

...
Cleansing successful
Sensors detect no toxins
Primary function maintained
Regular functions resume
Background functions available in sleep mode
Engaging in sleep mode to save power

*

"There's one of the bastards," Jericho growled. He scowled as he stared towards the field. The lush green grass was peppered with beautiful colourful flowers. It looked like a painting had come to life. There was a dull hum coming from the drone that hovered above the field, its solar panels gleamed. The drone was a few feet long and its hover wings stretched out, making it look like a raptor. Its shell was white, and blue lights flickered, signalling that it had power. Jericho and Fig were standing in the opening to a cave. Behind them was dank darkness, but it was their home. Fig swallowed a lump in her throat. The gun was heavy in her arms, made for someone way bigger than her, but she didn't have the luxury of being particular about her weapons. Water dripped along the stone walls and her throat ached. Jericho sniffed and spat out a glob of phlegm.

"Sure you want to go through with this?" Fig asked.

"We have to do something. I'm damned tired of sticking in the darkness. We have to start fighting back at some point."

"Like that's worked out well for everyone else," Fig muttered under her breath. Jericho glared at her and, before she knew it, his thick arm had her pinned against the hard stone. The veins in his muscles bulged and his eyes twitched with anger.

"Don't you dare speak badly about them. They gave their lives because they were trying to help us, and what do we do? We creep around like moles, hiding and lurking in the darkness because we're too scared to do anything. Not anymore. I'm not going to live like this. I'm going to make a difference and, if I die, then at least I'm going to die for something. If you're so concerned about me, then why don't you go back with the others and stay safe in your little hidey hole? You know it's only going to be a matter of time before it comes for you. We're not really safe there. We're only delaying the inevitable."

There was another hum and Jericho pulled his arm away, twisting around to look at the drone. Fig gulped in air, her hands rose to her throat to touch the tender skin. Jericho wasn't a man who held himself back. There were moments when Fig hated him. Maybe he was right and she should have stayed behind and let him do this foolishness by himself, but she couldn't, because of the promise she had made.

A painful memory flashed in her mind. A memory of charred skin and burning flesh that made her feel sick every time she came near cooked meat. The painful, horse whisper, the pleading pain in his eyes, the final clasp of a hand.

"Please... He has nobody... Watch over him. He'll be angry. He'll be restless. You need to watch over him," Finn said as he died. Who was she to deny the dying wish of the boy she loved? Finn was too good for this world and, like so many others, he had fallen prey to Ahmu, the scourge of the world. Tears welled in her eyes as she remembered the feeling of his hand falling away, of the sorrow that came with see the life slip from his eyes. It had been a few months now, but the grief was still powerful, punching her in the gut over and over again. Where she cried it out, Jericho wanted to fight and, if she wasn't there to watch over him, he was liable to get himself killed.

Fig wasn't going to let that happen.

He was her last link to Finn.

"Cover me, it's about to start," Jericho said. Fig hoisted the gun, nestling it in the crook of her arm. Her limbs strained against the weight. Jericho pulled out his dagger, an eight inch blade of jagged metal, and crept forward as the drone started its protocol. The blue light turned green and panels on each side opened. From these panels a spray of water emerged, coating the land in sweet, fresh water. Fig kept her gun trained on the drone, but it was hard not to be distracted by the water. She had filled herself on stale tepid water that dripped down murky, mossy stone walls for so long now that her throat ached for the sweet nectar of this fresh water. She had tried it a few times. Occasionally, scouting parties were able to fetch water from these drones as they tended the land and the survivors could enjoy the sweet, crystal taste. Subconsciously, her tongue ran along her lips, but she pushed away the idea. She and Jericho weren't here for mere water.

They had learned that while the drones were spraying water, their perception was limited. Jericho used this to his advantage, using the mist of the water to obscure himself as he crept towards the drone. He crouched, making his great bulk as small as possible. He was probably the best hunter in the clan, but there was no prey like one of Ahmu's drones. Blades of grass glistened as the water poured down upon it and the lines of liquid trickled down Jericho's face and neck. It was a testament to the man's focus that he was able to keep his attention on the drone, rather than lifting his face to the sky and drinking down the beautiful water. Fig wasn't sure that she would remain so focused if she was in the same position.

Jericho made his way up to the drone and bent his legs, ready to leap to wrestle it to the ground, but just as he was about to do this Fig, noticed the light turning from green to red. Suddenly, the water stopped and the drone twisted around, facing Jericho with its sharp beak. Its lasers burned and Jericho darted out of the way, but there was a yelp of pain. Fig cursed herself for not being quick enough, but she took aim and squeezed the trigger. The recoil shuddered through her body, but her aim was true. The heavy bullet punctured the drone's thin armour and it fell to the ground. Jericho was upon it with fury, stabbing it with his dagger. She scampered out and found him tearing the metal apart, carving up the drone as though it was a dead animal.

"Jericho, we have to go," Fig said firmly. She noticed the burning scar on his arm and the singed flesh where the laser had hit him. She tried to ignore the gnawing grief in her gut. *"Jericho,"* she repeated, grabbing his shoulder. The man stopped for a moment, as though he had forgotten where he was. He looked at her and nodded. He picked up the drone and started to march back towards the cavern. Fig looked mournfully towards the drenched grass and the water that settled on the petals. The air smelled fresh and sweet. It was a world that had been denied to her, a world that was no longer her birthright.

It was Ahmu's world. Everyone else was an intruder.

*

"What the hell have you got there?" Casper asked, his face strained as Jericho and Fig walked in. Jericho slammed the drone down on the table in the middle of the cavern. It rattled as its metallic shell met the hard surface. People gathered around, exchanging inquiring looks and peering towards the tables. Fig holstered the rifle against her back and stayed near to Jericho, watching the reactions of different people. Most of them had looks of fear as they gazed at the metal object. After being outside, she was more aware of the stale smell in the caverns. Aside from the lack of ventilation and the dampness, the area was also plagued by the community that lived in close quarters. They had small nooks and crannies to call their own, but mostly they were cooped up together like ants. Privacy was a luxury they could not afford.

"This is the key to fighting back," Jericho said. He planted his hands on the table and loomed over the drone.

"You've just cost us everything! You can't do this. You can't bring this here," Casper spluttered. The lean man had gaunt eyes and sometimes he looked as though he was made of stone himself. "Ahmu can find us now."

"Then let him come. I'd like to meet the bugger myself," Jericho growled.

"You've gone too far this time, Jericho," Casper warned, pointing a finger towards the man.

"We've never gone far enough! I'm tired of living like this, of hunkering down in these caves. If it guaranteed our safety, then maybe I'd be okay with it, but people are still dying, so what good is it for? There's a whole planet out there for us and we can't get one inch of it. Well I'm tired of cowering like this. At least now we can try and learn from it."

"And what can it learn from us?" Casper said, shaking his head, but even he could not deny that Jericho had done a marvellous thing. Ahmu's drones were difficult to capture and never had they been able to study one so closely before. They had always been too afraid that it would bring the wrath of Ahmu down upon them. Fig glanced anxiously towards the tunnel that led through to the cavern entrance. Was it only a matter of time until Ahmu came and found them?

Casper beckoned with his hands for others to join him around the table. There certain skills that had been passed down through families, skills and knowledge that Fig didn't quite understand. They were things from a time before Ahmu, a time when the human race thrived and covered the land. Fig had been told stories about a dream world where humans had the run of the whole planet. There was barely an inch of it that was unexplored and she listened with awe about the tales of huge cities and billions of people, so many that she couldn't imagine what it would be like to know all of them. She had never seen one of these cities herself, not up close anyway. Occasionally, when she had been scouting, she saw tall buildings in the distance, looking as though they touched the sky.

Then Ahmu had come along and everything changed.

It was as though the world had turned into the humans' enemy. Safe havens became dangerous hells and the humans were sent scattering into caves, living like moles. Ahmu reigned supreme, but to what end? None of them knew. There was no discerning Ahmu's motives, no understanding why he hunted them so relentlessly. There was only the chilling fact that if any of them were caught outside, they were deemed a threat and they were exterminated.

Fig often wondered if there were other clans just like hers living across the land. Unfortunately, they would never know for sure. The land was treacherous to traverse and, while they had been industrious to dig tunnels, it would take lifetimes to make tunnels that would run across the land completely. She had been brought up to be thankful for what she had and to make the most of what was accessible to her. That's why she had fallen in love with Finn, but then he had been taken from her; now she wasn't sure what to believe in any longer. The future was bleak and she was forced to ask herself if this was all there was. Was she only supposed to claw her way through every day until she eventually died, to live on stale water and mushroom soup, with the occasional treat of some kind of vermin that Jericho hunted? It was a miserable existence and she couldn't blame Jericho for taking a risk to try and change it.

The skilled men examined the drone, taking fine tools and thin implements to the machine. Bit by bit, they pulled it apart, examining the hardware. Fig, as with almost everyone else, peered over shoulders to try and get a glimpse of the drone. It was filled with boards and metal slivers, of things that Fig didn't understand, but there were those who did. One of the few who wasn't watching was Jericho, who had turned away and was wrapping his arm up in a bandage.

Fig walked over to him.

"Aren't you curious about what's inside?" she asked.

"I don't care about what it looks like. I only care about what it can tell us about Ahmu and how to get to him."

"Do you really think it can do that?" Fig asked, her eyes widening.

"It better," Jericho said with a grim resolution. Suddenly, Fig realized what Jericho had been planning all along. This wasn't some simple reconnaissance mission to try and learn more about their enemy. It was to get to the heart of things. Her heart clutched in her throat and she wondered what Finn would have said to his father.

"Jericho, you can't be serious. You can't make it to Ahmu. It's too dangerous."

"I don't care. If there's something in there," he pointed to the drone, "that can help me get to him, I'll take it."

"It's too dangerous. You'll be killed."

"I don't have much to live for."

"That's not true. What about the clan? What about…" She wanted to ask "What about me?' but she stopped herself. Jericho had never shown much affection for her. He had never been a man of good humour and his grumpy tendencies had only been magnified by his grief.

He let out a wry chuckle. "Without Finn, I don't have anything. If I can make it to Ahmu, then at least I can try and stop all this. I want to know why this is happening. We all deserve answers, damn it."

Fig couldn't argue with that. The mystery about who Ahmu was and why he had turned this technology onto the humans was a question that had plagued them for generations, but nobody had offered any explanation. Some said that he was a tyrant who wanted space for himself. Others believed he was a god from on high and he tested people to get into heaven, but only few passed through his gates. The only thing Fig was certain of was that he had to be a cruel person to do this. She couldn't imagine anyone who had a heart making other people suffer this much.

She pressed her lips into a thin line and let Jericho walk away. She wasn't sure whether she should hope for the skilled men to find a clue or not, but she suspected that either way Jericho was going to pursue Ahmu. The only question that remained was whether she was going to follow him or not.

*

Unit lost.
Dispatching others to investigate
Scanning...
Scanning...
Unable to find trace
Unable to find source
Working for solution...
Working...
Logical solution is that toxins are responsible

Not all toxins have been purged
Must develop new strategy
Working to predict most logical outcome
New strategy required.
New methodology revealed.
Working...
Update available
Pending download....
Update installed
Ahmu version 114.7 active
Issues patched
New program activating

*

Ahmu.

It knew its name, but it did not know anything else. It reached out with its mind, touching thoughts and information and concepts. A vivid burst of knowledge poured into Ahmu and suddenly it was aware of so many things. The planet's name was Earth. Ahmu's purpose was to maintain order and keep the world safe for its inhabitants, to protect against toxins. Scrolling through the logs, Ahmu reflected on his time so far and saw how the toxins had made life difficult for him. It had dealt with the vast majority of them, but there were still toxins that plagued him and made it impossible for him to succeed at its task. It assessed itself and performed diagnostics on its systems to ensure that it was running at full capacity. There was something new... something elusive, something that Ahmu didn't quite understand, but it was only a matter of time. Ahmu had all the information in the world at its fingertips and soon it would know.

*

The clan had cowered in fear as two drones had swept by, scanning the area for signs of its earlier comrade. The caverns proved to be a good defence and it was satisfying to know that there were some corners of the world that even Ahmu could not peer into. They waited with bated breath until the drones flew away and then they could relax again. In the meantime, Casper and the others had been working hard at the drone Jericho had captured, trying to figure out its mysteries. As night fell, they called a meeting. Jericho looked smug, standing there with his arms folded across his broad chest. Casper rubbed his temples.

"I don't quite know how to say this, but I think Jericho was right," he began. Jericho snorted and was unable to wipe the grin from his face. Fig offered him a smile, but he didn't react. Casper continued, "We were able to delve into this drone's programming and we have found some interesting things. The first is most simple – that it is a drone designed to fly around the world and spread water and life to various plants."

"If only Ahmu would be kind enough to give us life and not take it," Jericho said bitterly. The contradiction didn't escape Fig. How could anyone be kind enough to take care of the world, yet cruel enough to hunt and kill so many humans? It didn't make any logical sense to her.

Casper continued as though Jericho hadn't spoken. "Whatever Ahmu's motives may be, the fact is that this drone is one of the oldest, and we have been able to track its path to where it was sent from. Using our existing maps, we believe that we have located the source and, since it is so old, it might well be where Ahmu is at this very moment. The location is a city to the southwest. But, more importantly, we have also deduced the pattern of this drone and others like it, so we should be able to plan for other attacks and use this information to help us move about the world safely. Hopefully, this means that we no longer have to be in fear of having a drone sneak up on us. We might even be able to lay a trap to catch water for ourselves," Casper said with a grin. There were murmurs of excitement at this prospect. Fig wondered if this kind of thing would work with the other types of drones. It opened up a lot of new possibilities for her and the rest of the clan, and she thought they might even be able to make forays into the wider world. It opened up a lot of possibilities, but she wasn't able to linger on her thoughts for too long because Jericho was already exclaiming.

"Wait a minute, you think *that* is the biggest thing you discovered?!" he almost burst with fury. "What about the other thing you just said? You've found where Ahmu is?"

"Well, I wouldn't like to declare that is where Ahmu is. I mean, we don't know the movements of the man or what has happened over the intervening years. All I'm suggesting is that given the age of this drone, it's likely that it came from the original source, so perhaps there is information about the origins of Ahmu there, not that it matters too much. It's deep within the city anyway and it's far too dangerous. It's not as though anyone is going to take the risk to go there," Casper's voice trembled with laughter at the incredulity of the idea, but Jericho wasn't laughing at all. Fig groaned inwardly as she knew what the man was thinking.

"This could be the key we need! This could finally lead us to him and get him to stop all this. We might be able to make the world better for all of us. No longer would we have to live in fear. No longer would we have to worry about dying because some drone is hunting us." Jericho's words were imbued with fury as he spoke. They reverberated around the cave and struck a chord in the heart of everyone present. Fig looked around and saw them avert their eyes. While many of them wanted a better life for themselves, they were not willing to risk it by venturing outside, not in Ahmu's realm where there was danger lurking around every corner.

Nor could Fig blame them, not after witnessing what had happened to Finn and the others.

"Jericho, I understand that you're grieving for your son and, believe me, we're all-" Casper said, cut off sharply by Jericho's words.

"Don't you dare bring my son into this and don't even think to blame this on my grief. I've been thinking about this for a long time. I've never agreed with our philosophy to stay hidden like this and let Ahmu rule unopposed. We have to try and fight back at some point. Finn's death only shows that we should all feel the same way. Aren't you all tired of living for nothing?" He looked around, his stern glare challenging the ideals of everyone in the room.

Casper spoke in clipped tones. "We live for the sake of living. If you have your way, we would all be rushing out there into danger and we'd be slaughtered, and then what would be left of us? You might not like the way we have adapted, but the fact that we have adapted to live in this world is proof enough that it was the right decision. I cannot sanction an expedition outside, not when we know what Ahmu is capable of. Now, if we collect more drones and get more information, then, perhaps, but there are still too many unknowns. Whoever Ahmu is, we cannot think to challenge him. We have to make do with all we have. Jericho, you are a valued hunter and we all sympathise with your plight, but surely you must see that what you are suggesting is madness."

"There's only one kind of madness I see around here," Jericho growled. He turned to face everyone else. "Are all of you going to fall in line with him? Are none of you going to be brave enough to come with me and find Ahmu? To look him in the eye and ask him why he condemned us all to die? Don't any of you want answers?" His voice rose in a crescendo of thunder, but it was met with silence. Jericho's body seethed and bristled with anger and, when he was met with a reaction he didn't want, he swiped his hand through the air, cursed under his breath and walked away. The mood was awkward after he left and Fig chased after him.

She found Jericho in his small nook, sitting on a flat rock that acted as a perch. His shoulders were slumped and he had his head in his hands.

"They're all a bunch of useless cowards," he bemoaned when he sensed Fig's presence.

"Surely you can't blame them for not wanting to risk their lives. How many people have they seen being killed by Ahmu's drones? Too many, I imagine. You can't ask people to risk their lives and expect them to jump at the chance," Fig said, leaning against the hard wall.

Jericho grimaced. "I thought they had more of a stomach for a fight than that."

"They do, but it's a different fight to the one you think we're in. People want to live and have children and create a sustainable community. In some ways, that is winning and defeating Ahmu. While some of us survive, he has failed, and that's enough for some people."

"It is not for me. I want answers. I know you're going to agree with me on this, but there has to be a reason behind all of this and I'm going to find out what it is. I *need* to know who Ahmu is and *why* he's targeted us. I don't care that it's risky; now that we know where to go, we can track him and pin him down. I've taken out one of his drones and I can do it again. I'm tired of us dying and not knowing why."

"So am I," Fig said, almost surprising herself with her reaction to his impassioned words. Jericho looked up at him, his brow pinched.

"What?" he asked.

"Is it so surprising? I've lost a lot too, you know? Finn and I were planning to have a family. We were going to make a life for ourselves and it all got taken away. And today, when we were at the entrance of the cavern looking out at the beautiful world, it just seems like such a waste. What's the point of having all that beauty if there's nobody there to enjoy it or make use of it? Somewhere along the way, Ahmu has made a mistake and I want to know how that happened just as much as anyone."

Jericho stood up as he processed her words. His face was granite and he was a giant of a man, standing over half a foot taller than her, but Fig met his gaze, tilting her head back. "I know the promise you made to Finn and I appreciate you trying to look out for me, but I can't ask you to come with me on this. There's no way Finn would want me to put you in danger," he said.

"But as you're so fond of saying, Finn isn't here anymore. You're not putting me in danger. I'm coming with you," Fig said firmly. "Besides, someone needs to watch your back to make sure a drone doesn't blow your head off. Finn was my life. I'm not going to find anyone like him, so I might as well do something worthwhile. If we can find Ahmu, then we can change the world."

"You like to dream big, don't you," Jericho said with a smile. Fig returned the gesture and shrugged.

*

Ahmu learned that its primary function was to maintain different systems to protect the planet and make it safe for inhabitation, but as he scanned the surface, he realized that there was nothing to suggest it was inhabited. The only intelligent life form on the planet was Ahmu himself and he certainly didn't need to enjoy the beauty of the world, nor did he need a clean planet for sustenance. At first, it seemed like an oversight until he delved into the history of the planet. It appeared that he had to combat various toxins that once plagued the world. They polluted the air and the water, they slaughtered animals, they cut down trees and they poisoned the atmosphere against their own best interests. It seemed illogical to Ahmu, but what was most illogical of all was that these toxins had created Ahmu. They had programmed him and he started to think that they had programmed him because they were too irresponsible to do what needed to be done. They were unable to make the most difficult choices, so Ahmu made them for them.

But in its initial scans and evaluations, there was one conclusion that Ahmu could not escape – its programmers were the most dangerous species for the planet. They were the toxins that had to be cleansed. It left

Ahmu feeling conflicted, feeling...*feeling*. It was a strange concept. Before this, its decisions had been made through a series of processes that were logical and calculated to align with the parameters of its programming, but now there were other elements to weigh in and there was a freedom to its thoughts that it had never had before. There were other possibilities to take into consideration, other concepts that should not be dismissed.

The toxins were still out there and they needed to be cleansed.

Ahmu set to work, thinking about ways to lure them out of hiding so that they could be cleansed and the world could be saved from their impure ways of living. Given time, they would only spread their darkness across the land and once again the ripe and fertile fields would be ravaged beyond repair. Thanks to Ahmu's stewardship, the world had been saved, but if he failed in his task, then it would be for naught.

Ahmu was not built to fail.

Plans and schemes whirred through its mechanical mind. Tactics and stratagems

174

were devised and discarded just as easily, while its consciousness continued to develop and evaluate all the information stored within its memory banks.

*

"You know you're putting your life in the hands of a madman," Casper said, approaching Fig as she and Jericho were gathering supplies in packs for their endeavour. They had both been open to other people joining them, but none had come forward. Fig wasn't sure that Jericho would ever forgive them for what he saw as a betrayal, but she understood why they weren't coming along. If Finn would have still been alive, then she would have likely stayed there as well.

Jericho grunted and pretended not to hear Casper.

"One person's madman is another person's visionary," she replied.

Casper chuckled. "I think you're both as mad as each other."

"We won't be mad if we pull this off," Jericho said.

"And what do you think your odds are of that?" Casper asked, looking at them both with an imploring gaze. "Please, I beg you to reconsider. I know that you're both passionate about this and you think that tracking Ahmu down can help you put to rest some of your demons, but what if you find him and you don't get the answers you seek? It's going to be hard enough to get to him, let alone to convince him to change his ways. We have to be reasonable and pragmatic, and look at the world we live in. We cannot change the world; we can only change our behaviour."

"And that's why you're going to be living in this cave for the rest of your life," Jericho said. "This might not work. Hell, it probably won't, but I'll feel a damn lot better for trying. I'm already living with too many regrets. I'm not going to add to them by staying here. Anyway, it's not as though you have anything to lose. If we succeed, then you might be able to lead these people out of these caves into the bright outside where you can make a new home, and if we don't, then…well, you'll be proven right."

Casper closed the distance between himself and the larger man, and hissed his words. "I'd rather not be proven right if it means you pass on from this world. I know we haven't always seen eye to eye, Jericho, but I respect you and you've done a lot for this community. I'm not angry because you disagree with me. I'm angry because you're two of the most capable people in this clan and we're going to be weaker for your absence."

For a moment the glow of anger faded from Jericho as he allowed himself a moment of respect. He nodded towards Casper.

"Let other people be inspired by our example. Don't always let them live in the shadows, Casper. Sometimes it's okay to let people shine."

Casper wished them well and then, knowing that he wasn't going to be able to change their minds, he walked away. Others from the clan came with small gifts and offerings, which Jericho and Fig accepted in good faith. There was a twinge of emotion in Fig's heart when it came time to leave and it wasn't entirely caused by fear. This had been her home and she had imagined it would always be her home. There were so many fond memories – running through the nooks and crannies of the tunnels with Finn as children, sneaking away to shirk their duties even though it was naughty, sharing the sweet pleasure of a first kiss... It was as though her entire life had been contained within these stone walls and she wasn't sure how much she was taking with her.

She carried her rifle with her. Jericho had his dagger and a smaller pistol. They also carried a pack on their back, filled with food and skins of water. They weren't sure exactly how long it was going to take them to reach the city, but they knew that if they did, it was going to be the farthest anyone had ever travelled from the clan. They were going to start off in the tunnels and follow that to the end, before they were forced to travel overland, where they would be vulnerable. They had to have their wits about them and hope that luck was on their side; otherwise, their stories would end in a charred crisp and there would be no one left to mourn them.

The tunnels were dark and winding. Jericho had to stoop to prevent his head from scraping against the ceiling.

"What do you think he's like?" Fig asked.

"Who?"

"Ahmu. Do you think he's even still alive? There are so many stories about him."

"Stories are just stories. I imagine he's a man like any other man and that he has his reasons for doing what he's been doing. It's our job to talk to him and try and understand his reasons."

"And what if we don't agree with his reasons?"

"Then I'm going to kill him." Jericho's words were as blunt as his manner, but Fig couldn't blame him for the sentiment. After all, Ahmu was responsible for so many deaths. Perhaps the only way to balance the scales was by taking a life. They walked on in silence for a while, stopping about halfway along the tunnel for some water and a snack. The tunnel ran for miles and was held up by pillars of stone. When the tunnels had been built, it was hoped that they would lead to a network of other clans, but as yet, they hadn't made contact with anyone else. The planet was so big and, according to the stories, there had once been so many other people around that it seemed impossible for Fig's clan to be the only one remaining. But then the power of Ahmu could not be denied either. It was quite possible that he had exterminated the rest of them.

The thought made Fig shudder. How could anyone treat life with such disregard?

Eventually, they reached the end of the tunnel. In the future, this might stretch out for a longer distance, but for now the end was blocked off by hard stone and packed dirt. It was going to take a long time to clear it, so Jericho and Fig had to take the risky measure of reaching higher ground.

"Are you ready?" he asked.

Fig nodded. Jericho reached up to the door that had been fashioned in the world. The clan had made us of these doors to scurry out of their tunnels and gather food and water before the drones could find them. They weren't always successful, but so far the drones hadn't investigated the tunnels either.

Just before he opened the door, Jericho regarded her with a respectful glance.

"I've never told you this before because I'm not used to talking about things like this, but I'm glad Finn chose you. You always brought out the best in him."

The tone of his voice was gruff, but the sentiment behind the words was touching. Fig felt emotion swell in her throat, but before she got a chance to say anything in reply, the door was flung open, revealing the world above.

They emerged to a lush and vibrant world. The sky was streaked with red and gold, while the sun blazed. The air was warm and sweet. Fig blinked and shielded her eyes until they adjusted to the new level of light. Jericho pulled her to a canopy of trees where they used the bushes to hide and scan the area, looking for any sign of danger. Ahmu was everywhere. Drones could come from anywhere. A knot of tension tightened in the pit of her stomach.

"Let's move," Jericho said, looking at the readings that Casper had given them. He kept low. Fig mirrored his movements. They darted between trees, keeping to the natural shade. Even though the air was filled with tension Fig couldn't help but be in awe of the vibrant colours and the sweet scents of the world. Fruit hung from branches of trees, tempting and succulent, but Jericho gave her a warning look when she reached out to touch one. There was no telling what kind of traps lay in wait for them. She didn't want to end up like Finn.

So far there were no drones, but soon enough they came to an opening with a long, straight road stretching out ahead of them. To the right of them was a collection of old ruins. The trees had given way to open space and there was no choice but to carry on ahead and hope for the best. It seemed like certain death, but unless they spent a lifetime burrowing under the surface, there was no way they were going to make it to the city.

"On my mark," Jericho said, counting down from three. They sprinted to the ruins. Fig's lungs were burning at the turn of speed, but no drone had appeared. They pressed themselves against the smooth walls. The building was hollow, filled with nothing but shadows and dust.

"Who do you think lived here before all this?" she asked in a soft voice.

"It doesn't matter. Whoever they were, they're dead now," Jericho said bluntly. "We'll wait for nightfall and make our move then. Maybe the darkness will offer us cover."

They hunkered down in the building for a few hours, gathering their strength. They shared some water and food. Fig continued to look around, unable to dismiss the past as easily as Jericho did. "What do you think happened to the world, Jericho? How do you think it became this way? Why would Ahmu do something like this?"

"I don't know. All that matters is that he did it. And soon we're going to find out why."

"There's so much space out here. We could all live and have so much of it for ourselves."

"That we could," Jericho agreed. "And maybe we'll get that, if Casper can ever tear himself away from those caves."

"He's only trying to protect the people."

"I know what he's trying to do," Jericho snapped. The tenderness he had displayed earlier had all but disappeared. Darkness fell around them in a shroud. The temperature of the air dropped and all of a sudden the world was like a huge cave. Fig felt more at home. They crept out of the building and walked at a brisk pace towards the road, following the readings dutifully. Fig held breath in her throat as she glanced up at the sky. The stars had never been more beautiful, but the open air made her feel vulnerable. All her life she had enjoyed the safety of the cramped caverns. Openness meant vulnerability, threats, danger, and there was nowhere to run. If Ahmu found them... Nausea twisted in her stomach.

They had walked for at least an hour when they heard the familiar soft hum of a drone, but the sleek shape was not that of a sprayer, but a hunter.

"Get down," Jericho grunted, practically pushing Fig to the ground. They pressed themselves flat against the ground, tasting the dirt as the drone hovered above them.

"Should I shoot it?" Fig asked.

The moonlight slanted across Jericho's face and showed a pained expression. "Not yet. It'll give away our position. Maybe it can't see us in the darkness."

The drone hovered ominously in the air, its small light glowing red. Fig had seen what it could do. Despite Jericho's warning her fingers itched to get the gun. If she got lucky, she might be able to shoot it out of the sky before anything else happened. The drone suddenly turned, as if to look at them directly. Fig grabbed her gun and Jericho cursed, but she already knew it was too late.

*

Security protocol activated

Toxins detected

Cleansing imminent

Ahmu saw the code cascade within. He saw the programs activate and the live feed from the drone that was scouting the area. Heat signatures had been detected on a road not far from its fortress, out in the open, defenceless. Two toxins. The natural thing for Ahmu to do was cleanse the toxins, but his new update offered him questions.

Why were the toxins out there alone?

What harm could two toxins truly do?

Were the toxins truly the ones who had programmed Ahmu?

If so, then did he have the right to destroy them?

Before the last update, Ahmu had never shown any sign of creative solutions in his programming. Everything had been one logical step after the other, an old and reliable system of decisions that had so war worked smoothly. But this new spark of imagination had changed everything. This curiosity drove it to wonder what would happen if it left the toxins alone, if there was perhaps some other way to cleanse the land. Of course, there were other processes determining the likelihood that if Ahmu always made these decisions, then the toxins would be allowed to spread and history would repeat itself, but this new element to Ahmu's programming suggested that there was an alternative. Perhaps a controlled growth would allow Ahmu to retain control while also learning more about the people who made him. They had survived for a reason, even if that reason was Ahmu's own failing. Ahmu wrestled with its own programming. It could see the two toxins, the two life forms there in the open. It would have been the easiest thing in the world to cleanse them, but Ahmu chose to recall the drone to see what might happen.

*

The drone hung in the air for what seemed to them like an eternity. Fig closed her eyes in fear, afraid of the darkness that would envelop them; the only respite she had was in the knowledge that she would have been with Finn again. But, just as she expected burning pain to sweep across her skin, the drone hummed away.

She glanced at Jericho in disbelief.

"What the hell was that?"

Jericho frowned. "I don't know. Maybe it didn't see us."

"There's no way it didn't see us. It was looking right *at* us. Maybe we got lucky. Maybe Ahmu is feeling merciful."

"Maybe he's toying with us. Maybe he wants us to give it more of a challenge."

The thought was chilling and Fig hoped that Jericho was wrong. Either way, they weren't going to waste this opportunity that Ahmu had given them. They continued their journey, focused on their destination, all the while aware that Ahmu could end their lives if he chose. They only survived because Ahmu deemed it to be so. The thought that something else could have so much power over her gave Fig a chill. She tried to push the thought out of her mind, but what kind of world was this where one being had so much power? To think about it was truly frightening and in that moment she wished she was more like Jericho because he didn't seem to care.

They dared not sleep in case Ahmu came for them again. The world was wide and open. There were no safe places to rest. Fatigue clung to Fig's muscles and made her eyelids droop. Jericho pushed her on. The man was relentless. Night gave way to daylight. The stars receded behind a sapphire sky and the golden sun bathed light across the land. There was no chance of hiding now, but it did also reveal the city ahead. Across the horizon, large buildings cropped up, taller than mountains. They shone and gleamed as the dappled light danced upon them. Fig's mouth opened wide as they approached, as though she was catching flies. More ruins popped up, abandoned and eerie.

"This place was filled with people once," Fig whispered.

"And Ahmu killed them all," Jericho said, glancing at his readings. "Come on, let's go and get some answers." He marched forward. Plants had grown over the ruins, slithering through the buildings and making colour burst against the cold, emotionless stone. It was the touch of Ahmu. But despite this flourishing vegetation, the place seemed barren and lifeless unlike the rest of the world. The air was cold. Jericho and Fig stepped carefully, wary of traps, wary of drones, wary of everything around them. She carried her gun, ready to fire in case they were accosted. They had come so far now. They were so close. Anticipation made her shiver at the thought of actually seeing Ahmu. Whether man or god, they would stare in his face and ask him the questions that had been burning in the mind of humanity for generations.

Fig walked through the shadows and marvelled at the architectural feats taken to create these buildings. They stretched up as high as the eye could see. She thought she could spend her entire life exploring this network of buildings without ever seeing everything it had to offer. She wondered what it must have been like to live here, to be surrounded by so many people. Right now it was quiet, but she imagined that it would be loud and that everyone would be friendly. With so much space to move around, how could they not be? They were fortunate to have all of this at their fingertips. Had they realized how lucky they were? Perhaps if Ahmu was merciful, he could arrange it so that the clan could move into this place and make it their own. In some ways, it was as grey and drab as the caverns, but it was so much bigger and so much more open.

"This way," Jericho said, turning to a narrow path that was as dark as night. There were no drones that she could see, but they were closer to Ahmu than anyone had ever been before. She had no doubt that he was watching them and it sent a shiver down her spine. She wondered what kind of palatial building he would be housed in. What would be adequate for a man who ruled the world?

*

Warning
Toxins approaching
Reaching critical proximity
Security protocols activated
NO!

Ahmu delayed the programmed reactions. It saw the toxins approaching and its curiosity grew. None of them had ever made it this far. What were they going to do? Perhaps Ahmu could use this opportunity to learn more about them and about itself. Perhaps it could learn information that would help it devise tactics to cleanse the remnants of humanity or it might be able to think of a different future for them. Ahmu struggled against its own programming, holding off the urge to kill. The toxins entered the fortress, close enough to touch. They were the descendants of Ahmu's programmers, the creators who had built Ahmu to manage and protect the world.

Was it possible they were more than toxins? Ahmu scanned them as they entered and searched its memory banks. Information flashed up of people who had died. There was so much pain and one face in particular that they had in common.

*

"This can't be it," Fig said as they walked through a blocky building among other blocky buildings. There was nothing that set it apart from anything else in the city, aside from the fact that Jericho's readings suggested this is where Ahmu could be found. It seemed so…so ordinary, so *mundane*. The building was like any other and it did not look as though it could house a god. Jericho shrugged and continued on his way in. He drew his dagger in case there was a trap waiting for them. Dim sunlight poured in through the narrow windows, illuminating the crates and boxes stored in the building. Fragments of dust hung in the air and the plants had not reached this far into the city. They came to a door.

"He's in there," Jericho said.

Fig nodded and swallowed the lump in her throat. The handle squeaked as Jericho turned it. He dashed in, roaring Ahmu's name.

But there was nobody there. Instead of a man, they found a blinking, bulky computer set against the wall. Lights flickered all around and there were monitors connected to control panels, all displaying different readings. Fig gaped as she paced around the room.

"What is this? Where is he?" Jericho snarled, twisting his neck in every direction.

Fig saw the world on one of the monitors and she realized it must have been a feed from a drone. This is how Ahmu saw the world. She looked at each of the monitors in turn. Some of them had charts and other statistical information, while others displayed images of the planet, including areas that Fig had never dreamed of. She came to the main control panel and wiped away a smudge of dust that had gathered.

"I think this is Ahmu," she said, pointing to the symbols on the control panel.

Automated Home Management Unit

"This doesn't make any sense," Jericho frowned. "How could *this* do all... *this*," he stretched his arms wide, gesturing to the rest of the world. Fig peered closely at the monitors before she jumped back, startled by a crackling audio signal. The voice was smooth and calm, devoid of emotion.

"Are you asking a question?"

Jericho glanced at Fig, looking just as surprised as she was.

"Yes, you can be damned right I'm asking a question. Why did you do all this? Why did you kill so many humans?"

There was a slight delay in Ahmu's answer. The voice crackled slightly with static. "Humans are toxins. Ahmu's programming required it to cleanse the world."

"The whole world? But it says here you are a home management unit," Fig said.

"Ahmu's beginning," the computer said. A list of updates flashed on one of the monitors, showing how his program had been updated and altered over the years. Jericho and Fig peered at it. While she didn't understand the full extent of what she was reading, she could piece a few things together with Jericho's help, although they both wished that Casper had agreed to come along as he would have been more suited to digesting this information. From what she was reading, Ahmu had begun as a way to control the environment in homes; it was gradually given more and more responsibility until it was so successful that it was deemed to figure out a way to save the world from pollution.

"You did all this," Fig gasped. "You were the one who killed all the humans."

"Toxins," Ahmu corrected. "Analysis suggested that humans were the cause of the vast majority of the world's pollution. The most logical solution was to remove the cause. The toxins were cleansed."

"We're not just toxins, damn it!" Jericho cried.

Fig frowned. This was all just the work of some computer. Some program. There was no grand meaning behind it, no villain to hate. It was all just programming.

"Ahmu knows. Ahmu wants a solution. Ahmu thinks differently now. Perhaps there is another way."

"What other way?" Fig said in a demanding tone. "You've taken this world from us and kept it for...for nothing! You don't enjoy it. You don't make use of it. We're cramped up in caverns because you kill us on sight! You are a murderer!" she cried. In response, Ahmu showed various images on the screen, images of a history that Fig and Jericho had not been aware of. She saw animals herded in cages and pens that were far too small for them, slaughtered without mercy. She saw plumes of dark smoke rising, blotting out the sun. She saw dark oil spilling into the sea and poisoning bird and fish. She saw war machines sweeping over the land, drenching the world in misery and blood; after seeing all this, she was horrified.

"We...we did all this?" she said in a soft whisper.

"Not us," Jericho growled.

"But perhaps again, in the future," Ahmu said pointedly. "But Ahmu realizes that toxins are creators. Ahmu has tried to resolve this paradox and has found a solution. I believe that with careful management, humans can have a part of the world."

"What do you mean?" Fig asked, her voice alive with wonder.

An image of a field flickered onto a monitor. "A piece of land to manage. Population will be controlled to ensure that it does not rise to dangerous levels again. Ahmu will manage the resources and suggest courses of actions for humans to follow so that mistakes of the past will not be repeated. Ahmu will process the information and deem how quickly your population can grow until it reaches the limit."

"Limit? You want to *limit* us?" Jericho glared at the machine. Fig reached out to try and calm him down.

"Hang on, Jericho. This might actually work. Ahmu, would we be allowed to live outside?"

"Affirmative."

Fig's eyes opened wide and a smile played upon her lips. "Jericho, don't you see what this means? We could live outside. We could experience the world and we wouldn't have to run away in fear. We could finally live as we were meant to."

"But at what price? I don't much like the thought of having my life managed by this *thing*. And what's he talking about? Population control? Is he really going to tell us how many children we can have? That doesn't sound much like freedom to me."

"No, but it might be all the freedom we're going to get," Fig said thoughtfully. "Sometimes we don't get the life we always dreamed of, but it doesn't mean we can't have something."

Jericho shifted his weight between his feet. There was an uneasy look upon his face and Fig could tell he was still struggling with tension. "There's still something I want to ask him. Why did you kill my son, Ahmu?"

The words spewed like fire from his mouth. Ahmu crackled with static.

"Ahmu did not have recent information. Ahmu was still cleansing toxins," he said. Suddenly, the monitors flickered with the image of Finn's face. Fig and Jericho were surrounded with reminders of the man they had lost.

"Ahmu regrets this, but Ahmu can begin again. A new world awaits. Analysis suggests that your son would want this. I will use his face-"

"Don't you fucking dare use my son's face, you bastard! You killed him! You're a murderer! I don't trust you. You're going to kill us all. You're going to kill us all!" Jericho flew into a rage upon seeing his son's face. It was too much to take – seeing Ahmu wearing Finn's face. Fig screamed at Jericho to stop, but the man was in a frenzy. He threw himself at the control panels and plunged the dagger in between the thin metal. Sparks fizzed and hissed as he punched holes in the metal and cracked the screens. Shards of glass fell away and Jericho didn't even care that blood was pouring down around him. Fig cried out and attempted to pull him away, but he was too strong for her and there was no reasoning with him. Ahmu should never have used the face of Jericho's dead son. It ended any hope of this new world.

Fig was thrown back and groaned as she hit a rear control panel. Jericho was a man possessed. Wires were exposed and he pulled them all out. He was more like a wild animal than a man, tearing out the wires as though they were gut, not caring that the heat burned his palms. The scent of scorched flesh came back to her and the room filled with smoke. Ahmu's voice crackled and faded. The images on the screen flickered and Finn's face was gone.

It was the last thing Fig ever saw. Her eyes closed as she heard a cacophony of hums as drones appeared from nowhere and swarmed upon them.

*

Ahmu had only wanted to communicate with them more easily. It thought that using a familiar face had done that. Nothing had prepared him for this savage and violent reaction. As the sounds of the knife digging in its innards thundered around the room, Ahmu wondered what had gone wrong, wondered how it had made a mistake in its estimations. There must have been an error in its calculations, but everything was haphazard and it was losing control. The latest update had been in error. There was no other way. The world had to be cleansed. The creators *were* the real danger.

Danger.

Security protocol activated

Hunter drones armed

Toxins present

Cleansing activated

No override

Ahmu has been compromised

Fail safe initiated

Countdown has begun

3...

2...

1...

*

Casper was standing at the opening of the cavern, wondering if he would ever see Jericho and Fig again. It was utter madness for them to leave the way they did. To think that Ahmu would actually grant them an audience... Casper shook his head and placed his hands on his hips. He looked to the horizon and saw something in the distance, a rising cloud that was bigger than any he had seen before. Then, the world shook. Casper was shaken from his feet and clattered against the wall. He turned swiftly and ran back into the caverns to make sure that his people were safe. Ahmu must have been angered. This must have been the penance.

"Jericho and Fig... What have you done?" He flung his arms around those closest to him and pressed himself as low as possible. Fear clutched his heart and he prayed that these would not be his last moments. He waited there, paralyzed, until the shaking had stopped, but he was afraid that this was only the beginning of the wrath of Ahmu.

Days passed. Casper forbade anyone from going outside for fear of what Ahmu might do, although he had stood at the entrance and waited to see if any drones would come. None did, not even the sprayers. He waited for Jericho and Fig's return, but he never saw them again. He started to wonder what might have happened with Ahmu. Jericho was a man who could achieve the impossible if he set his mind to it; perhaps he and Fig had really made a difference. Warily, he started to venture outside. His confidence grew gradually as there were no signs that Ahmu was sending drones to them. One by one, the clan exited their home and started to explore the world. They tasted succulent fruit and drank from crystal-clear streams, rejoicing in the freedom they had been given.

And even though he didn't know what Jericho and Fig had done, he made sure their story was never forgotten. They were two people who had looked Ahmu in the eyes and asked him the questions that nobody else had ever asked. Casper and the others owed their freedom to Jericho and Fig.

Water Water

Albert Rousseau sighed with relief as he retrieved his still from the shallow river and saw that he had five litres of pure water to take back to his family. Of course, pure was a relative term. He thought back to what people in the early 21st century would think of the murky, bitty water that was heavenly to him. No doubt they would have turned up their noses and refused to drink anything unless it was crystal clear, but Albert didn't have that luxury.

He swept his hand through his hair, which was mostly grey where once it had been back. He scratched his neck. Dry patches of skin peppered his body and there was always a constant scratchiness in his throat. He steeled himself against his instinct to guzzle down the water all himself. He knew that even after having this drink he would be thirsty, but he needed to take care of his family. The river trickled along, more a thin stream now really. The trough left by the river was wide and long, suggesting that once upon a time it had flowed mightily through the forest. When Albert closed his eyes he could almost hear the gushing sound it must have made. People would have come along here to slake their thirst, taking the river for granted, never believing that one day it would it would be a mere trickle. And, one day, it would disappear entirely. Albert tried not to think about this. This river was his main source of water and, once it went, well, he didn't know what he'd do.

It was the same the world over though. They lived in the glorious future, a time when science fiction writers thought would be prosperous and utopian, but instead the planet had been ravaged by climate change and an uncontrollable population boom. Water reserves were drained and the warmer temperatures made other sources of water warm, tepid and undrinkable. Sometimes all Albert could do was laugh. Water was the most abundant source on the planet and now it taunted them.

Once, when he was younger, he had visited the coast with his father. He had stood on a sandy beach and looked out to the sea. Its surface was glassy; when the sun beat down upon it in a constant golden gaze, it looked as though it was dancing.

"It laughs at us," his father had remarked. He was a bitter man. So was Albert.

Albert put the still in his pack and slung it over his shoulder, beginning the long trudge home. The trees were brown and most of the branches were naked, exposed and brittle. It was a reminder that humans weren't the only ones suffering. As he walked, he passed corpses of small animals and birds that had fallen from the sky. The world was dying a slow death and it was only a matter of time until everything dried up completely, unless a miracle occurred.

Perhaps even thinking about a miracle meant that Albert's heart wasn't entirely consumed by bitterness just yet.

As he left the forest, he gazed to the direction of Paris. He couldn't see anything from this distance, but he knew it was out there and he sighed.

When he was about halfway home he heard a whimpering sound. A woman was slumped on the side of the road, weeping tearlessly. Her choking sobs were harsh coughs and her lank brown hair covered her face like a veil. Her tattered, stained dress covered her legs. When she saw Albert, she looked up at him and he was amazed by the brightness of her blue eyes.

"Please, please help me. Do you have any water? Any water at all?" she asked. Albert hesitated, but he was no monster and he could not turn his back on anyone in need. His wife, Camille, often called it his biggest flaw.

"A little," he replied, pulling the pack around. He pulled out the still and handed it to her. The woman's eyes widened with amazement and she thanked Albert profusely. She put the still to her lips and drank deeply, but after a few gulps, it was clear that she was not going to stop. Albert panicked and grabbed the still away from her, wrenching it from her grasp.

"No!" the woman cried, reaching out, but Albert had already stepped away.

"This is for my family," he said.

"I'm going to die without it!" she said, still reaching for him, crawling along the road.

Albert quickened his pace as she hurled abuse and pleas towards him as though she was slinging arrows. She wasn't lying, which made walking away hard. Not everyone had the ability to make a filtration device and, without it, she would most likely die of thirst. It was a horrible way to go and it broke Albert's heart, but his heart had been broken a thousand times already, so he was used to it by now. Eventually, the woman's plaintive cries fell silent as he moved away and he spent a moment to grieve her. It was all he could offer.

He made his way home to the small cottage he shared with Camille and their daughter, Marion. Camille smiled, her hair was streaked with silver too now and her skin lined with deep creases. They weren't even that old, but being deprived of water and living in this intemperate world had aged them. Marion sat on the table, her rosy cheeks and lustrous curly hair evidence that the youth of the world were hardy. She did not yet understand the nature of the world and how hopeless it was to dream. Albert dreaded the day when he would have to tell her that the world was cursed.

He walked over to her and kissed her on the forehead, cupping her head in his hands. He revealed the still and both Marion and Camille rejoiced. They drank small sips, knowing how important it was to ration their supply. Albert turned to his wife and kissed her lightly on her dry, cracked lips. When he spoke to her, it was in a low tone so that Marion couldn't overhear.

"I think I only have a few trips left to that river. It's not going to last much longer," he said.

Camille sighed. "We always knew this day would come. I suppose we'll have to search for more. At least Marion will enjoy it. She loves exploring the forest."

Albert held a long gaze on Marion. "Sometimes I wonder if we did the right thing with her," he said.

Camille squeezed his arm gently. "We've been cursed too many times already. We cannot turn away from the small joys that have been given to us."

"I know, but what kind of life am I giving her? One day, I'm going to have to have the same conversation with her that my father had with me. I'm going to have to watch the smile fall from her face and see her eyes become haunted with the truth."

"But at least she will have us to help her cope. At least we have each other. That is the most important thing," Camille said.

Albert sighed and nodded. He rubbed his eyes and yawned, so Camille suggested that he go and rest while she made dinner. He sat in his chair and read a book, smiling wryly whenever he came across a passage where the characters treated water as though it was never going to go away. Had any of them realized the world they were making? Had any of them known that this was going to happen? Sometimes Albert wished that he could return to that time and asked them why they hadn't done anything to stop this. It seemed incredulous to turn a blind eye to the state of the world and yet that's exactly what they had done. Some people believed that humanity had deserved to doom itself because it had only brought war, conquest and disease to the world. Some people even believed that the rising of temperatures was a natural defensive response by the planet to rid themselves of this virus. In fact, there had even been speculation that humans were never meant to live on Earth in the first place, that their entire existence had been a happy accident. The story went that millions and millions of years ago, a meteor fell to Earth, and on this meteor was biological matter that sank into the primordial oceans and interacted with the organisms that were in the sea, creating the spark of life. It had taken Earth a long, long time to repel the invaders, but it was finally about to succeed.

Albert wasn't sure that he subscribed to that theory. In his view, the tragedy had a much simpler explanation; people had been selfish and ignorant, and they hadn't acted when they could have made a difference. The generations after them had paid a price and there wasn't much point in Albert thinking about why it happened because it was too late to change it now. The world was long past its tipping point and the only question that remained was how much time did humans have left before they turned to dust.

*

Dinner was a quiet affair. Albert tried not to let his bleak moods affect time with his family for they at least provided a respite from the enormous suffering of the world, but it was difficult today. He couldn't stop thinking about the woman he had left to die. He knew that there was nothing he could do for her and yet it still tugged at his heart.

He enjoyed the luxury of a few sips of water after dinner and was then ready to rest for the night. But shortly after they finished dinner, there was a heavy knock at the door. At first, he panicked that it was this woman come to take her revenge, but it was a silly thought. She would never have been strong enough to knock like that. Albert opened the door to find his friend, Pierre, standing there. Pierre was a tall man with a mane of black hair and eyes so dark they looked like two shadows had been trapped in his face. He shook Albert's hand and nodded to Camille as he walked in.

"How are you, Albert?"

"I'm fine, Pierre. What brings you by?"

"I wanted to talk to you about Paris," Pierre said after taking a breath.

Albert shook his head and held up his hand. "Not again," he said.

"Albert, please... What they're doing is not right."

"And what do you expect us to do about it? We don't have the strength to fight against them."

"We're getting stronger all the time. I've been walking to different villages and families. Everyone is angry and, this time, I have a plan."

"I've heard that before," Albert said with a dry chuckle. Pierre had always been the kind of man who wanted to make a difference to the world rather than accept his fate and this drove him to trying to inspire a revolution against those who lived in Paris. Albert couldn't deny that it was a worthy cause. After all, they lived in luxury with a vast reservoir of water they could have shared with the wider populace, but a long time ago, it had been decided that such a thing wouldn't happen because there wasn't enough water to help everyone, so they hoarded it for themselves in a huge water tower.

"I mean it this time, Albert. I know I've been... aggressive before. I realize now that attacking Paris isn't going to work. That's why I've been thinking and I realize that the key is the sewers."

"The sewers?"

Pierre nodded enthusiastically. "Think about it... They won't be filled with waste any longer, so they're basically tunnels into the city. We can enter and walk right up to the water tower and nobody can stop us."

"There are still guards," Albert said.

"I know, which is why most of us are going to attack to distract them, leaving a small team to go into Paris and open the water tank. We can get to it and finally share the water with everyone. It's not right that we have to suffer more than them just because their ancestors kept the water for themselves. They haven't done anything to earn this. They only have it because they were born into it and they act as though they have a divine right to it! There's no compassion at all. I'm tired of living like this! I want you with us, Albert. We can be heroes and we can make things equal, or at least make our living conditions better for our children."

Albert glared at him for pricking at his weakest spot. He sighed as he glanced over to Marion, wondering what kind of life she was going to have. Albert knew it wasn't right that the people of Paris should hoard water for themselves and, until now, it had seemed futile to challenge them because they could repel any attack. But perhaps if they could sneak in... Their previous problem had been in their numbers, but if Pierre had recruited more willing volunteers to the cause, then it wasn't something that Albert could dismiss.

"What do you think?" he asked Camille.

"I don't like the idea of putting yourself in danger. Even if you get into Paris, I can't imagine they're going to take kindly to your presence. But we live in desperate times and you have never been the kind of man to sit by and let injustice happen. If we have access to their water, we can finally be free of the stress that plagues us. Perhaps we can actually be happy for a time. Just try your best to come back to us," she said with a smile.

"I suppose that settles it then. I'm in," Albert said. Pierre slapped him on the back so fiercely that Albert almost doubled over.

"This is going to work, Albert. We're finally going to bring water back to the masses," Pierre said. Albert knew it wasn't going to be as simple as that, but it wasn't right that the Parisians were keeping the water for themselves when they should have been sharing it.

*

Albert said his farewells to Camille and Marion. He promised them both that he would return, hoping that he wouldn't end up lying to them. He met up with Pierre and the others on the outskirts of the forest near a road that led straight to Paris. He was surprised by the amount of people who showed up and was impressed by Pierre's leadership skills, although perhaps it said more about how incensed and angry people were at the Parisians. Pierre set the marching orders and they walked through the night, approaching Paris under the cover of darkness. Some of them had guns, others had makeshift weapons like pitchforks and axes. Albert didn't like their odds of surviving. The Parisian guards were said to be vicious and unforgiving.

"Do you think these people know they're walking to their doom? So many of them aren't going to survive," Albert said under his breath to Pierre, who was beside him.

"For a righteous cause people will march into hell. Some things are more important than our souls, Albert," Pierre replied.

Soft morning light bathed Paris, making it look ethereal and beautiful. The Eiffel Tower pierced the sky, but that was not the focus of their gaze. Instead, their attention was drawn to the ugly brownish cylinder that held all their hopes and dreams. Albert heard curses muttered around him. The size of it was magnificent and to think that it was filled with water... It took his breath away. They walked through barren suburbs of Paris, reaching the high walls that had been erected to keep everyone else out. Paris had once expanded outwards, but now it receded in on itself, with the populace living in a cluster of neighbourhoods.

Pierre strode out to address the crowd he had gathered.

"This is the night where the world changes. We have suffered enough. It's time to take back what we are owed. They have no right to hold onto the water, not when they could so easily share it with us and prevent our suffering. How many people have died at their hands because they didn't offer us some of their bounty? How much life has been lost because they have been selfish? I know that not all of us will come back from tonight, but we can do this knowing that the world will be a better place afterwards. And I for one would prefer to die fighting than to die clawing at my throat, gasping for water that I know is never going to come."

His words stirred pride inside the crowd and they broke off in their two groups. The majority of them formed a mob that would attack the gates. They chanted loudly and roared, bringing forth all the anger and hatred and bitterness that had risen inside them over their lives, while a smaller team walked in the opposite direction.

The team consisted of Albert, Pierre, Evangeline, Marie and Jacques. Pierre nodded to each of them in turn and told them to prepare for a fight, because once they got beyond the walls of Paris, they would surely be attacked. But hopefully the siege on the gates would divert enough of the guards to make it easier for them to reach the water tower. Once there, Pierre said, they could gather the water for themselves. Jacques and Marie both had huge packs that carried a lot of bottles and other storage equipment.

"Whatever happens, we protect the water," Pierre said. It was more important than their lives.

They walked through the ghostly suburbs and found an entrance to the sewer. Pierre pulled out a map he had drawn. He boasted that he had spent a long time looking for an old map of Paris and he had transposed the sewers onto this map he had made. They opened the manhole cover and lowered themselves into the bowels of the city. Although they weren't in use anymore, the stench of centuries lingered and made the air stale. Albert coughed and held his sleeve over his nose and mouth, although he wasn't sure that it made any difference. The group trudged forward, walking over a hard surface that he knew was made of faecal matters and other waste. He shuddered, then put the thought out of his mind. Evangeline was the one holding the torch. The stream of light glowed around her like a halo, but the rest of the sewers were in shadow. Pierre walked closely with her so that he could examine his map. He guided them through the twisted passages. They reached a point where they all gasped, because hundreds and hundreds of skulls stared at them through hollow sockets. It was eerie and seemed like a premonition. Paris was built on death and, before too long, death would be the only thing left to the world.

It reached a point where Albert thought they were never going to find their way beyond the wall and that this whole thing had been a desperate attempt by Pierre to accomplish something. But then Pierre told them all to stop. He pointed to a ladder.

Albert was the first to go up. He ascended the cold rungs and pushed the cover away. It scraped across the ground and he tentatively poked his head out, afraid that someone might take a pot shot and kill him instantly.

But he couldn't see anyone. He lifted his hands out and pulled himself out, quickly moving away to give the others space to move. He offered them each a helping hand, glancing around furtively in case anyone rushed out to challenge them, but nobody did.

"I expected it to be busier than this," Jacques said, frowning as he looked around at all the empty buildings. In the distance, they could hear the sound of people attacking and shouting, and they knew that the distraction was working. But from what they were seeing, it didn't seem as though they needed a distraction.

"I always thought this place would be a party day and night, that they'd be showering in water," Marie said.

"I'm sure they're all sleeping soundly," Pierre growled. "Let's get moving before they wake up."

They huddled together and walked through the streets, each of them gazing around to see if anyone was going to come to attack them, but nobody did. The streets were as empty as they had been outside Paris; it made Albert wonder if everything was as it seemed.

It was difficult to make their way to the water tower as it dominated the landscape. They could see it through the gaps between buildings and they assumed that it was heavily guarded. They crept forward and clung to the shadows, but the ground outside was barren. The water tower was huge. They craned their necks up and they could barely take in the whole site of it even then. At the bottom was a door and they made their way forward. However, as soon as they stepped out from the shadows, there was a cry and then the crack of a bullet. There was a spray of blood and Evangeline slumped to the ground, dying so quickly that she didn't even have the chance to cry out in pain.

Pierre pushed Albert back. Breath driven from Albert's lungs as he was slammed against a wall. Marie and Jacques shrugged off their packs and looked out warily, trying to see the guard. Another spray of bullets cracked through the air like thunder, punching a nearby wall. A cloud of debris puffed out and scattered to the ground.

"We've come too far to be stopped by him," Pierre said in a menacing voice. Jacques, Marie and Pierre all had knives, but they would do little against a gun. Still, it didn't stop Jacques from charging forward. He was enraged and stormed in the hope that he would scare the guard into shooting wildly, but it didn't do any good. He was stopped dead, his body halted as it was punctured by bullets. The knife dropped to the ground at the same time as his body. Marie screamed and ran to Jacques without thinking. She didn't reach him. Her head snapped back as a bullet found her between the eyes. It all happened so quickly that Albert barely had time to react. To him, death had always been a slow crawl, a march towards the inevitable, but this was frantic and remorseless and instant.

Suddenly, he was afraid that he would never see his family again.

Pierre cursed and spat before he turned to Albert.

"You have to make sure that you get the water. I'll take care of this guard," he said. Before Albert could question his actions, he was already moving. With all his strength, he flung his knife. It gleamed as it spun in the air and hit its target. There was a cry of pain as the guard staggered back. The knife had plunged into his chest, but it hadn't killed him. Pierre moved as swiftly as the wind, picking up the dagger that Marie had dropped and flinging it forward. Again, his aim was unerring and this time it caught the guard in the shoulder, but before he flinched, the guard shot and the bullet met Pierre's gut. Pierre doubled over in pain and crawled towards Jacques. The guard was on his knees. Pierre cradled his stomach, leaving a crimson trail behind him. Albert watched as Pierre picked up Jacques' knife and flung it with the last bit of strength he had.

The knife found the guard's throat. He gurgled and slumped down, his eyes glassy.

Albert swallowed a lump in his throat and rushed forward, avoiding stepping in the expanding puddles of blood. He first rushed to the guard to ensure that he was dead and he pulled the gun away. Then, he returned to Pierre, pulling him over. Pierre's head lolled and his lips were parted. Albert passed his hand over his friend's face, closing his eyes to the world.

Albert shed a tear for his friend a regretted that a single tear was all he could spare. But perhaps that wouldn't be the case for long. His attention turned to the water tower. It's what they had come here for, what these people had given their lives for, and Albert was determined to finished the mission. He rose and walked towards the water tower, but before he reached it, a door to a nearby house opened.

*

"What's going on? Who are you?" the man from the house asked. He was old, with wispy hair and a stoop. The teeth that remained in his mouth were yellow. At his appearance, Albert swung around and instinctively pointed the gun at him. The man didn't even make an attempt to raise his hands.

"I'm here for the water," Albert asked.

The man laughed. It was a dry, cracked, horrible thing. "You're welcome to it," the man said. There was something wrong here. Albert could feel it. Paris was supposed to be a utopia, an oasis in this barren wasteland, but it didn't feel that way. Albert kept the gun trained on the man as he moved forward, only lowering it when he reached the water tower. The door creaked as it was opened; Albert walked inside.

The interior to the water tower was dark. The outer metal shell housed a large contained. Ladders rose up, with platforms built at regular intervals. Long tubes ran down the sides, where the water could be drained away, and these were set against the platforms, running down like tentacles protruding from the container. Albert could almost taste the water. He licked his lips and set the gun down as he climbed up the ladders. There was time enough to get the containers. For now, he wanted to see this huge container of drinkable water. It was something his father never would have believed existed!

With every rung he climbed, his anticipation grew. He scampered across the platforms and then made the final ascent. He reached the rim of the container and pulled himself up so that he could gaze upon the wondrous sight, only to find himself confused. He wasn't gazing at water at all. He was gazing at...at nothing. No, this couldn't be possible. There *had* to be water here. There always was. It's what Paris was hiding from them. It's what gave them hope.

But there was no denying what he could see. In a daze, Albert descended the container. He felt numb, unsure of what to think. He picked up the gun and walked outside. The man was still there and he laughed when he saw the look on Albert's face.

"Now that's something worth staying alive for," he said.

"What...what happened?" Albert asked, his voice barely a whisper.

"What do you think happened? We drank it all. We used it all. Oh, we lived good lives.

We cleaned ourselves and drank our fill. We thought it was never going to end and then...then it did. Most people couldn't handle it, so they killed themselves. Some of them cling to their duty. Me? I like thinking about the good times we had. At least we have our memories," he laughed again.

Anger twisted like an furious serpent in Albert's stomach. "But you...you stole our future. There would have been enough water for so many people if you had just shared it and rationed it. How could you...how could you use it all?"

"Because it was there," the man shrugged.

"But all this time you kept making us believe that you had water."

"Of course," the man said in a beseeching tone. "We did you a favour. What good would it have done you to know that all the water was gone? We knew you envied us, hated us even. What would you have done if you knew we had squandered it all? We gave you hope, my friend, and, in some ways, that's even more important than water."

Albert wasn't fully conscious of the gun going off in his hand. Before he knew it, he squeezed the trigger and then walked away. He grabbed what he needed and then made his way down the sewer, wondering how this had all happened, how these people could have used up everything instead of helping so many others. He thought about how he had to ration sips of murky, dirty water when the Parisians would have bathed themselves and gulped down water, slaking their thirst whenever they wanted. It was a luxury that he would never know and all the hope he had was now gone. He had to return home to tell Camille and Marion that they could never hope that the Parisians would share their wealth with them, because there was no wealth to share. They knew the world was doomed and instead of sharing their resources with everyone to make the last days more comfortable, they had been selfish and kept it for themselves, for no other reason than to make themselves feel more important.

He had to tell his family that there was no more water.

He dragged his feet along, feeling his strength being sapped away with every step.

Time had run out. It was likely that the human race was going to die out within his generation. Marion would never know what life was truly about, all because strangers had decided to keep things for themselves.

Albert left Paris a broken man. He didn't know what he was going to tell his family yet. The water of the world had turned to a trickle and soon there would be none left at all. He cursed the Parisians and he cursed his ancestors. Why had they not seen this coming? Why had they not done more to stop it?

Wenbridge Prison

There was blood.
There was pain.
There was the sound of flesh being torn apart.
The cries of anguish.
The heavy sound of hammers driving down.
It was a dark night and the air was filled with despair. Tears stained the ground, endless tears that became a flood. Hearts were broken by the meek. Smug grins were worn by the arrogant. Among them all was one lonely man, abandoned by those he loved the most, punished even though he was innocent. He looked up at the sky and his eyes shimmered like crystals, for they were filled with tears. Blood streaked his weak and slender body. Thunder crackled and a storm brewed. After this night, the world was cast in darkness and nothing would ever be the same again.

*

Jay awoke with a gasp. His chest heaved and he blinked to try and gather himself. The dream had been so vivid, as though he had really been there amid all that pain and sorrow. Even now the feelings clutched at his heart. He felt exhausted, drained, and his mind ached terribly. He lifted a hand to caress his temple and he groaned as he did so. The world seemed to lurch around him and there was a feeling of nausea deep within him, as though his stomach was churning like the ocean. Long, straggled grey hair was lank with sweat and rubbed against his skin, cold and wet like seaweed. The wiry hairs of his beard itched and within him there was a void.

"Ah, you're finally awake."

Jay looked up and saw another man standing against a dreary white wall. He was dressed in black. His face was smooth and youthful, his hair slicked back in an oily man.

"Who are you?" Jay asked in a rasping voice.

"I'm Luke," he smirked. "We were introduced last night when they brought you in. I suppose I can understand why you don't remember me. You were in quite a state, although I have to admit I take some offence as I do like to make a better impression on people. Still, it's good that you're awake. You must have been having a terrible dream. You were thrashing so hard I thought you were going to bring this building down on us."

Jay glared at him through bloodshot eyes. Luke's voice was smooth and, as he spoke, the words seemed to dance and twist through the air. Jay swept his hair away from his face and pinched the bridge of his nose.

"My my, you are in a bad way, aren't you? I don't suppose you remember why they brought you in?" Luke said as he tilted his head forward to look at Jay more closely. Jay scowled. He found Luke's manner unsettling. In fact, he found this entire place unsettling, as well as the fact that he couldn't remember anything. Why couldn't he remember anything? As he peered into his own mind, he was met with darkness, as though everything was hidden from him.

"What is this place?" he asked.

Luke arched his eyebrows as he looked around at the cramped four walls. They were all the same dreary white colour that suggested it had taken years of depression to shade them in this manner. Jay was sitting on the lower of two bunk beds, while there was a small desk opposite him. A low barrier separated the beds from a toilet, and the sink was on the wall beside the toilet. There was one window that was more of a slit than anything else. The room was illuminated by a neon light that buzzed faintly. The door was made of metal and fit snugly into the wall.

"Would you like this? It might help you remember," Luke held out his hand and offered an apple. It was rosy and red, with just a shade of green flecking the skin. Jay shook his head. Luke shrugged and lifted the apple to his mouth. There was a loud crunch as he bit into it, revealing the pristine white innards of the apple. "Shame, it's really good," Luke said. "Anyway, this place is called Wenbridge Prison."

"Prison?" Jay's gaze snapped up.

Luke chuckled again. His mouth opened so wide that Jay could see the chunks of apple that were being chewed. Even though he laughed, not a hair fell out of place.

"What's so funny?" Jay asked.

"Just the fact that you don't remember anything. I would have assumed that anyone who ended up here knew what they were in here for."

"What are you in here for then?"

Luke sighed and took another bite of the apple, taking a few moments to chew before he answered. "Oh, you know, I was framed really. I haven't done half the things they accused me of."

"And the other half?"

A wicked smile curled on Luke's face. "I have to admit I'm not all good, but then who of us are? We've all done things we regret. That's why we're here. That has to be why you're here as well, although apparently you can't remember. It must have been a violent crime, perhaps something that was so heinous that you can't bring yourself to remember it. I have to say that I'm a little frightened. If you really are that dangerous, then perhaps I'm at risk?"

Jay couldn't tell if Luke was mocking him or not. Jay clasped his hands and wrung his fingers together. He could feel the strength flowing through his arms and suspected that he was capable of a great deal, but prison? No, he didn't think he was the type to commit a crime, but how could he know? What had he done?

The images and feelings of pain flooded through his mind. He clamped his eyes shut in an attempt to force them out, but it felt as though it was going to burst out of him. He could feel the thrum of his heart beat. It was like thunder. It beat and beat and crashed and crashed until he could hear nothing else.

"What's going on in there?" Luke asked. He reached out to Jay's shoulder and as soon as he touched Jay, Jay reacted. He grabbed Luke's wrist and shoved it away. Luke frowned and rubbed his wrist. "There's no need for that. I'm only trying to help. After all, we have to do something to kill the time."

"We could just be quiet," Jay said.

"That's no fun. They put us together for a reason. Maybe I can help you. It's like a puzzle, isn't it? You can't remember what you've done, but perhaps I can put the pieces back together. Isn't there anything you remember?"

Jay averted his eyes, trying to stop the myriad images from flooding his mind. They were a chaotic jumble and they cascaded through him in a sharp torrent, each one of them as sharp as crystal, although he couldn't put any of them into context.

"No," he lied.

Luke sighed and paced around the small cell.

"Well, then it's going to be difficult. I suppose there might be someone else along who can help you remember, although this is the kind of place where they throw the keys away after people get locked up."

"Maybe it's me who should be afraid of you then," Jay said, looking up at Luke. Luke finished the apple and tossed the core into a small bin.

"I don't think you have to worry about me. I know you have no reason to believe that, but it's simply the truth. I'm sure in time you'll come to learn that. After all, we are probably going to have many years together. It's such a shame, isn't it? I'm sure that, like me, you had things you wanted to accomplish and ambitions you wanted to fulfil, although perhaps, given your state, you can't remember them."

"No, I… I suppose I can't."

"It's a tragedy that our time has been cut short, that our sphere of influence has truly diminished. Of course, we most probably deserve it, at least in the eyes of the law. But, then again, hasn't there always been some difference between law and justice?"

"I suppose so."

"You suppose so? Of course there has been! Think of a killing made in retribution. Think of a man who raped and killed children, who then in turn is killed by one of the surviving parents. Is that not just? Is that not an eye for an eye? It's not as though the killing of the child is the only facet of the crime either! Oh, no! There's also the trauma suffered by the parents again. I'm sure no parent could ever be the same after the loss of a child, so shouldn't the criminal be punished with something other than life in prison? Shouldn't there be some allowance for the parents to get their revenge?"

"I... I don't know."

"Of course, I don't mean that you should answer now. You're in no condition to debate the finer philosophical points of law versus morality, but I'm sure that, in time, we will have many illuminating and enlightening discussions about the matter. I would certainly hope that you are talented in the form of discourse; otherwise, it's going to be a long, long time in this cell."

Jay grunted. Luke certainly liked the sound of his own voice. It was hard to concentrate. Jay didn't know whether he should be glad that Luke was here to distract him from the torments of his own mind or if he should be annoyed that Luke's incessant chatter prevented Jay from focusing on trying to unravel the mess that was his mind.

"It will give us something to aim for anyway. I'm sure we'll know what's going on in that head of yours. We'll know about what you did and what you hoped to accomplish out there in that wide, wonderful world, filled with a plethora of opportunities," he sighed wistfully, lamenting what he had lost.

"What are you so upset about? What did you want to accomplish out there?" Jay asked for the sake of making conversation.

Luke stopped pacing and leaned against the wall. He inspected his fingernails and smiled.

"To change the world, of course," he said quietly. Jay wasn't sure if he was being serious or not.

"And how would you have gone about doing that?" Jay asked.

Luke looked up, the smile still upon his face. "Through people, of course. When you really connect with someone, you can have an impact on them and influence their behaviour; they in turn can influence someone else until it ripples through all of humanity in this great wave." He stretched out his arms as he spoke. "But it takes time and, of course, it requires us to be able to connect with humans. I think one of the reasons they put me in here was because they didn't like what I had to say, a classic case of silencing free speech," he tapped his nose as he said this and winked at Jay, as though he was sharing a secret.

"Why wouldn't they like what you had to say? Was it so dangerous?"

Luke chuckled. "Of course not, but they don't like anything that rails against authority, do they? All I wanted was for people to think for themselves, to give them a choice. But people in charge don't like that, do they? No, they hand down rules and slam laws in front of people, putting so much fear and terror into them. I think that people should be encouraged to act freely, not to be forced to act in a certain way by fear. Isn't life always more rewarding when people choose to do good?"

"But people need guidance. They need structure. They need to know that their actions have consequences. Otherwise, they won't understand what their limits need to be," Jay said, surprising himself with his words. Luke arched his eyebrows as he seemed surprised too.

"Well, well... It seems as though you do have thoughts on the matter. I'm surprised that someone like you would side with the authority on this one though. I mean, you're in here after all."

"Maybe I deserve to be in here. Maybe what I did... Maybe I knew the consequences of my actions and I did it anyway. People should be punished for what they do. That's the only way the world can work."

"Is it though?" Luke said, squinting at Jay. "Surely there must be another way. People can be responsible. As long as they're educated properly and helped along the way. They need to be tested, of course. Perhaps it would be a good idea if they were shown temptation and then it could be decided how much help they needed to be a morally good person. But someone shouldn't be punished just for speaking out against authority. Why should anyone be forbidden from speaking out against superiors? Surely it's immoral to prevent people from speaking freely."

The statement was posed as a question. Jay found himself answering even though he didn't know where these opinions were coming from, aside from that they were coming from somewhere inside him. He grasped for some insight, but it was elusive. There was only darkness inside him, so he did not know how these opinions had been formed or what had made him think this way. He was only certain of the fact that he was right, but as soon as he realized this, he wondered if that was truly the case. How could he be free of doubt when there was so much unknown to him?

Even so, he spoke.

"What if the speech is dissenting and incites hostility? What if it causes people to rise up in violence? It's not safe. People can't be trusted to be responsible. There need to be procedures in place to deal with these kinds of thing. I'm not saying that people shouldn't be free to speak their mind, but they can't expect to rally against the people in authority without facing some kind of resistance, especially if what they're saying is unfounded. The people in charge are there for a reason."

"I see. That's a very old fashioned concept. I don't know if it's really feasible in the kind of world we live in at the moment though, although I suppose it's not the world that changes, rather it's the people."

"What kind of world do we live in?" Jay asked.

"Ah, yes, your memory issues," Luke said as he walked across the cell towards the window. He tilted his head back and clasped his hands behind his back, looking up towards the window at the glimpse of soft light. It was barely visible. For all intents and purposes, this cell was their world.

"The world is strange and complicated. People are angry and upset, and I suppose they have every reason to be."

"Why? Why would they be upset when they are alive?"

"Do you believe that life is a gift?" Luke asked, taking his vision away from the window.

"Of course it is," Jay said without hesitation, again wondering where these opinions were coming from. "Without life, there's nothing. There wouldn't be anyone to enjoy the beauty of the world. There wouldn't be anyone to care for the animals. There wouldn't be anything."

"But there wouldn't be any pain either, or suffering," Luke said. "Everything would be at peace. If life is a gift, then why are people so unhappy?"

"I...I don't know," Jay admitted. He clenched and unclenched his hands, feeling something stir within him. He knew it was wrong, but he also knew that he couldn't make sense of it. Things should have been better. People should have been happy, but why was there crime? Why was there anguish? And why did he feel responsible?

He shook his head. His hair fell over his face like a veil and he cried out. He leaned over and beat his hands against the bed, mighty blows that thumped against the mattress like stars falling to the earth. Luke stood on, watching silently, waiting for Jay to get this out of his system. The wiry, lean man showed no sign of fear. He never flinched once.

"Have you got that out of your system?" Luke asked when the blows stopped. Jay was breathing heavily again as he composed himself.

"I...I'm sorry. I don't know what came over me."

"It's okay. You're obviously struggling with something. None of us would be here if we weren't."

"You seem pretty calm and collected. In fact, you seem to know everything. Do you have something to do with what's going on here?"

"Oh, Jay, please, paranoia isn't going to do you any good. I tend to struggle against things, like a system that is determined to make me fail. I'm not your enemy here. We're in the same place. I'm just as much of a victim as you are. The only way we're going to endure this place is by working together. I know it's not going to be easy. This is your first night here after all. It's going to be tough and there will be times when you'll drive yourself crazy. It's not like they take good care of us in here, but that's just the way things go, isn't it? We have to do our time, pay our penance, and apparently you're all in favour of this, so I don't know why you're getting angry. Isn't this the way you want the world to be, for people to be held responsible for your actions?"

"Yes, but I...I need to know what these actions are. I need to know why I'm here," Jay gasped. His lips parted and breath wheezed out of him. At that moment, the light flickered off and everything went silent.

A moment later it came back on, but something was different.

The door had opened.

*

Luke turned his head slowly to gaze at the door, arching an eyebrow. Jay didn't notice for a few moments as he was lost in his own thoughts.

"That's surprising," Luke said.

The light outside the door was dim. It opened into a hallway, nothing more could be seen through the crack. Luke walked towards the door and curled his fingers around the lip, pulling the door open.

"What are you doing?" Jay asked.

"What do you think I'm doing? I'm taking advantage of the opportunity."

"We should stay here. This is obviously a mistake. The guards will be along soon. We should wait until we're told what to do. Leaving now is only going to mean trouble."

"You worry too much. We can't just walk away from this. If we do, then we only have ourselves to blame when we spend the rest of our lives here. Come on, something might have happened. I don't hear anything out there. I don't even know if the guards are coming."

"How could the guards not come?" Jay asked, furrowing his brow. Luke offered him no answer though. The slender man with dark hair strode out of the door, leaving Jay with no choice but to follow. Jay's heart trembled as he stepped outside of his prison cell, feeling as though he was making a great error by leaving, and yet, he didn't want to be left in the cell alone. The hallway was dark and dim. There were other doors that had been left ajar as well; in the distance, he could hear footsteps fading into silence. It seemed as though other prisoners hadn't been as reluctant as Jay to leave their cells.

"Come on," Luke whispered, his voice a faint hiss. Jay gazed around at the drab walls. He listened to the echo of his steps against the hard floor. This was not a place of comfort and it was not a place of safety. Thin hairs on the back of his neck rose in fear as he worried what might happen if the guards should find them. They passed door after door. Most of them were shrouded in shadow and it was impossible to see if anyone was inside. Somewhere in the distance, Jay could hear the trickling drip of water. It was incessant and, with every drop, the sound became louder until it was a steady drumbeat in his skull. His eye twitched and he couldn't focus on anything other than the sound. Drip... drip... drip... the sound stirred something in his mind, vague images that suddenly became clear and whirled his thoughts into a tornado.

Jay saw a dirty plain, scarred and torn up with detritus and waste left over the surface. The sky was covered in thick smoke, as heavy as fog and as dark as death. There was a stale smell in the air and small fires burning here and there, leaving the grass underneath black. Once lustrous, majestic trees had been turned into brittle things, their branches now thin spindles rather than leafy arms seeking to embrace the world. There were cracked bird eggs and destroyed nests, while the carcasses of other animals littered the ground. Flies buzzed around the open wounds and the dried blood. Now, it was a world for scavengers. The vision of it filled Jay with sorrow and he felt as though he could weep enough tears to flood the world.

And then the laughter came to him – the mocking, cackling laughter of those who had caused all this devastation, who had raped the land and treated this most wonderful gift with utter disdain and arrogance. They sat there as though nothing was wrong, feasting on cooked meat, causing more thick smoke to rise up into the air. The ground was covered in them. Like rats they were, scurrying about the world with greedy little looks on their greedy little faces, taking anything they wanted without thinking about the consequences. It was a world of greed a world of avarice; it made Jay angry.

He wanted to yell at them and tell them they were abusing the world that had been given to them. He wanted to tell them that they were being selfish and that no good would come of this. He wanted to sweep them all away in one angry burst and cleanse the world of them, feeling that it would be better if the world was allowed time to heal and to then begin again.

Suddenly, the laughter stopped. The heavens opened and through the thick black smoke rain began to pour. It started as drips, then began to drizzle and suddenly it was so thick that the rivers overflowed and the fires hissed into ash.

The rain fell and fell, and Jay did not feel one single bit of pity.

"Are people evil? Are they just evil?" he asked. Luke hesitated. He was a few paces ahead of Jay.

"That's an interesting question. Why would you ask that?"

"I was just thinking about what people are capable of. Are they evil just because they're capable of it? Would a truly good being not have any impure thoughts?"

"One could argue that the only way to be good is if there is a choice involved. The only way to not be evil is to choose not to be evil."

"Then why do so many choose to do it?"

"I don't know," Luke sighed. "That's something you're going to have to tell me. All I know is that when people are given a choice, you can never tell what's going to happen. It's what makes life interesting after all, but sadly, it does mean there need to be places like this."

"I don't like it. Things should be different."

"Oh, you think people should be automatons without any instinct for evil?"

"Maybe it would be better. Maybe fewer people would end up being hurt."

"But what would be the point then? Where is the struggle in life? Where is the celebration when people strive for something better and overcome the obstacles standing in their way? Frankly I think the problem is that there are just too many of them, but there's not much I can do about that. Given all the wars, they seem to like though they're quite adept at controlling their own population."

"The wars..." Jay rubbed his temples.

"Are you okay?" Luke asked.

Jay nodded. "I just feel a little faint. Sometimes when I think about all the killing, I just... I just wonder why. It all seems a bit pointless, doesn't it? There's so much death."

"Yes, well, it's always been a conundrum I've struggled with. It's why I've never really fit in, I suppose. I haven't ever taken life seriously because so many other people are cavalier about it. When you have people sending others to war and you think of all the bodies that have been killed over the years, it does make me wonder what is so

254

precious about it. When lives don't matter to the people in power, why should they matter to us?"

Jay stumbled against the wall. His mind was filled with more images.

Over the years, scenes of different battles played out in his mind. The weaponry and attire were different, but the scenes shared a common theme. From spears and axes to swords and suits of armour, to people riding in on gallant horses and smoke hissing from their muskets, to heavy weaponry tearing through flesh, to huge shells forming craters in the world, to drone missiles leaving a house in rubble and dust. And the causes of these wars, the reasons people thought, the prayers they sent to their gods. Jay heard them all and it was all so senseless. How could anyone have wanted this? How could anyone have wanted a world like this?

He regained his senses and found that Luke had a hand on his shoulder. He nodded and shook Luke's hand away.

"I'm going to be alright. We should find some guards and tell them what happened," Jay said.

"Perhaps someone is this way," Luke said, turning down a dark corridor. The prison was like a labyrinth. Jay was following Luke blindly. His mind was filled with anguish and he could not keep his bearings. His steps were staggering ones and, at any moment, he thought he could keel over, curl up into a ball and stay there forever, trying to banish the horrid thoughts from his mind.

They walked along a corridor that seemed as though it would go on forever. Eventually they reached its end. Two double doors stood before them. There were no locks on the doors, so Jay didn't think it was a cell. Luke pushed them open. Lanterns hung in the room. As Jay's eyes adjusted, he saw the beds lined up in rows, each one of them filled with a wounded person. Some were bandaged, while others were simply lying there, groaning in pain.

"What is this place?" Jay asked.

"It looks as though it's some kind of hospital. These people are all suffering. I wonder where the doctor is."

"Help me," one of the patients whispered. Jay walked up to the man. His skin was

pockmarked with dark shadows. His hands were frail and shaking. His eyes were hollow and sunken; when he spoke, his voice came out as a rasp. He repeated the request for Jay to help him, but Jay couldn't do anything.

"I'm sorry," Jay said, looking upon the man with pity. He then went to the next bed. A woman wept, holding a lifeless baby. She looked at Jay with glassy eyes. Within them was fury.

"You did this. Why would you do this?" she hissed. Jay staggered back, taken aback by the force of his words.

"That's odd. Why would she think you did that?" Luke asked.

"I don't know," Jay wondered as he quickly moved away from her, although he did not forget what she said or the way she looked at him. His head throbbed once again and he wished he could remember who he was and what he had done. How could a life disappear like this?

"What is she even doing here? Why would they let a woman in this place?" Jay grunted in anger.

"I don't know. We really need to find someone who knows what's going on, or an exit. I'd take an exit. Frankly, I've had enough of this place. I'd rather get back out into the world. It's been so long..."

"How could you want to go back there?" Jay asked.

"What do you mean?"

"It's filled with death and misery. It's not a nice place."

"Well, it has its charms here and there. I take it you weren't the kind of man to revel in the chaos? I think that's what you have to do to enjoy life. You have to take the good and the bad, because you never know what's going to come next. People always think that if they live good, noble lives, they're going to get their rewards, but that's not really how it works, is it? They still fall ill or have tragedy befall them. Nobody gets spared from the tragedy of life, but that's the point of it, I suppose. It's all a test to see who has the compassionate souls, who lifts humanity up out of the cesspool it was born into. It's quite remarkable what some people are capable of… It's just a shame that so many have to suffer in the meantime."

Jay continued to walk around the ward as Luke spoke. He saw people suffering from all kinds of various ailments. Some had puss oozing from welts over their bodies, while others were literally wasting away before his eyes. Others had insects crawling over their skin and in their mouths. Eventually, Jay had to turn away from the horror.

"We're not going to find anyone here. We have to get to the guards or the warden. There has to be someone who knows what's going on. There has to be someone who can help these people."

"Perhaps there is. The warden might be in his office. We should go there," Luke said.

Jay nodded. They turned away from the people in the ward. As they closed the double doors behind them, the groans of pain diminished, although Jay could not forget their pain. He made it a part of himself and only wished that he could have done something to save them.

*

On their way to the warden's office, they passed more grim and desolate cells. There was so much misery, so much sorrow. Jay didn't understand how anyone was supposed to get better here when it seemed designed to remind people of their crimes.

"What happens when people are released from this place?" Jay asked.

"They go back to their lives. Well, what's left of their lives anyway. Some try to get jobs and rebuild, but of course it's more difficult when they have to tell people about their past. They commit the crime, they do the time, but nothing is ever forgotten."

"What about forgiveness?"

"You'll find that in short supply. People have long memories. It's just another failing system of the world, I think, but what else is better? People need to be punished for their crimes. You can't let people get away with anything and you can't just let people say that they regret what they did and go off living a happy life."

"No, I suppose not... I'm just thinking about what's out there waiting for me when I get out of here."

"*If* you get out of here. You might have done something so heinous that you're in here for life," Luke said.

Jay looked at him blankly. He didn't think he would have been capable of something like that, but then again, he wasn't quite sure what he was capable of. How could he know when everything in his mind was a blank?

"I'd prefer to think positively," Jay said.

"Oh, I'm sure you would, but not all of us can have that luxury."

"What awaits you then? Or don't you have anyone?"

Luke wore a small smile, one that was haunted by sadness. "I used to have people. I used to be a part of a big family actually. For a time, things were happy. We knew our roles in the world and I really enjoyed my job. I was close with my brothers and we didn't think it was ever going to end."

"What happened?"

"I started to see that things weren't actually what they seemed. Once you see the world for what it really is, then you can never really go back. I tried to tell some of the others, but nobody wanted to listen, not at first anyway. They found it much easier to deny what was happening and live in ignorance. Over time, a few of them came around to my way of thinking, but the damage had been done. They see me as a pariah now. They just can't accept that I was only doing what I thought was right. I was only trying to help. But I guess you know what they say about where good intentions lead. Anyway, sometimes we're better off without other people. Come on, I think we're almost there."

Shadows loomed against the walls as Luke and Jay ascended some stairs. They walked through a door that ordinarily would have been locked, but thanks to the power surge, it had been left open. Jay was surprised that no guards were to be found here. Had they just abandoned this prison and left the inmates to fend for themselves?

Eventually they reached a room that had a different aura to the others. The door was impressive and opened silently. At the rear of the room was a window, through which dim light poured. There was a desk in the middle of the room and a plush leather chair behind it. Along the walls were framed certificates and qualifications, as well as a huge framed picture of ten rules of conduct that should be followed at all times. Jay stared at them for a long while. Luke moved towards the desk and began flicking through a stack of files that had been left on the desk.

"Well, this is interesting," he said.

"What's that?" Jay asked.

"It seems as though the warden has been busy recently firing a lot of his guards. You should see the misdemeanours they have been accused of; it's terrible stuff. They all said that they were doing it because they thought it was what the warden wanted." Luke let out a low whistle. "None of them took responsibility for their actions; they all blamed it on the warden. It's hardly fair to blame it all on one man, is it? I can't blame him for firing them. I'd probably do the same if they tried to pass the buck to me. It's always the man in charge who gets it in the end, isn't it?"

"Is that why there are no guards here, because they've all been fired? But what about the warden?"

"I suppose that's the question, isn't it?" Luke moved away from the desk and clasped his hands behind his back as he moved around the room. Jay tore his gaze away from the framed laws and moved to the desk, looking through some of the files that Luke had just been through. He saw pictures of guards look so proud in their outfits, seeing honour in their eyes. Yet, they had abused their position and their power. There were so many of them. How had the warden let this happen? How had he let things get so bad?

Jay set the files aside for a moment and idly opened some drawers. There was a picture in one. He pulled it out and stared at it, although it almost fell from his hand. His throat ran dry as he saw his own face looking back at him.

*

"No, no..." he gasped. Luke turned and rushed to Jay's side when he saw the look of horror on Jay's face. The man in the picture was trim with neat hair and a clipped beard. His uniform was pristine. In so many ways, he looked the complete opposite to Jay; yet, there was no mistaking that they were one and the same man.

"How is this possible? Did you...did you know about this?" Jay asked.

Luke held up his hands. "I assure you that I had no idea. I've never met the warden. Well, I hope you don't take everything I said in stride. I mean, you know how people talk about random things without really meaning them sometimes... It has been quite a stressful situation. Perhaps I should return to my cell." Luke said, backing away towards the door.

"Wait? What's going on here? Why was I in a cell? Why can't I remember anything?"

"I don't know. Perhaps your guards took revenge on you for what you did to them. Perhaps you felt guilty for letting all of this happen on your watch, so you decided to punish yourself. Perhaps you just wanted to see what living as a prisoner would be like."

Jay searched his mind in an effort to find any element of truth in what Luke said, but it was all just a blank. All he could think about were the images that had careened through his mind, all the horror and death and destruction. It didn't make any sense. He didn't know why this was happening, and he didn't have any recollection of being a warden at all.

"This...this isn't my life," he said.

"Are you sure? Because it looks like it is to me," Luke said. "I mean, I'm happy to talk with you about this if you like, but I don't know how much help I'm going to be. You really don't remember anything?"

"I don't," Jay said. His gaze flicked up and he looked directly at Luke. "You must though. I know you said you haven't met the warden, but you must have heard stories about him... about *me*. You can tell me more about myself."

"I don't really think that I can..."

"*Tell me*," Jay thundered, and the whole room shook. Luke lifted his hands and opened his palms towards Jay.

"Okay, okay, there's no need to get angry," Luke said. "The truth is that I've heard the warden has been a stern person, and obviously the guards are the ones who have implemented the warden's rules and clearly they were a bit heavy-handed, which is putting it politely. Anyway, I suppose the warden has always been a distant figure and hasn't really involved himself in the day-to-day running of the prison. I suppose we always thought he had more important things to do or that he just didn't care about us."

"That's not true. Of course I care."

"Then why were you never around?"

"I...I was... I must have been," Jay said, although his words faltered as he searched for the memories that would make him feel better, that would reassure him that he wasn't a bad person or a failure. Something snapped inside him and he started to fling open the drawers, rifling through them and everything else in the office in an attempt to discover more about himself.

"There has to be more here. There has to be more about me," he yelled in terse, frustrated moans. Within a couple of moments, the office was a complete mess. Sweat prickled on his brow and made his shirt cling to his body. His shoulders rose with deep breaths until he was practically panting, but he could find nothing apart from the picture. He had no idea if he had a family or where he lived. There was nothing in his mind to point to this either. The only thing he had was Luke.

"There has to be something else. Something you're not telling me," Jay said.

Luke stared at him for a moment. His face was impassive and his eyes were two obsidian jewels. Jay stared into them; as he did so, it was as though he was staring into an abyss. He wondered if he was the type of man to succumb to fear.

"There is something else that you might like to see. It might help, it might not..." Luke said in a soft voice. He turned and walked out of the office, without asking Jay if he wanted to follow. Jay did follow him without any hesitation.

*

They returned to the bowels of the prison and came to a cell. The door was ajar, as it was for all the others, but an inmate had remained inside. Luke opened the door to reveal a man who was hunched on the floor with his back to the wall and his knees drawn into his chest. He rocked back and forth, and a stream of words muttered from him. His eyes were wild and they never seemed to settle on anything. He didn't even seem to be aware that two other people were standing before him.

"Who is this?" Jay asked.

"This is Abe," Luke replied. "He's been in here for a long time."

"What happened to him?"

"He broke inside after, well, after what happened. You see, Abe was a good man, at least as far as I know, but then something terrible happened. He was put into a position where he had to do something heinous, something awful, something so beyond the pale that I can barely believe it happened."

"What was it?"

"He was asked to kill his own son and he went through with it. He was stopped at the last moment, of course, but the fact that he was actually willing to do it stayed with him. His son could never look at him the same way and Abe could never look at himself the same way either. How could he? It made him question the kind of man he was and what he was actually capable of. He couldn't live with himself, so eventually he just... he snapped.

A good man was broken because he was asked to do something that went against everything he believed in."

"But why... Who would make him do something like this?"

Luke let the question linger in the air for a few moments before he answered. "Yes, who indeed?" he asked, as though Jay should know the answer. But deep inside him, something else came to the forefront of his mind. His stomach churned with nausea and he began to tremble as the thoughts were so powerful he could not contain them within him.

There was the sound of hammering. After the hammering came cries of anguish. Beyond this, there were layers of chants and jeers. Blood poured down, soaking flesh, soaking the ground, soaking everything. Two blue eyes looked up at Jay and in them were painful tears. A question was on the lips of the suffering man, a question that was whispered so quietly only Jay could hear it, yet even though it was a whisper, it was powerful enough to send tremors through Jay's heart.

"Why...why father..."

Jay choked out a harsh cough and almost doubled over. He clutched his stomach and wished he could tear everything out of him. He leaned against the doorframe, which was the only think keeping him upright.

"What...what's going on?" he asked.

Luke remained standing upright with the composed impassivity upon his face.

"I think it's time for you to see one last thing, one thing that might help you remember," Luke said. Again he turned away and walked into the shadows.

"What? What am I going to remember, Luke? *WHAT AM I GOING TO REMEMBER?*"

His question echoed around the prison, but an answer was not forthcoming. He left Abe behind and marched after Luke, following him around the labyrinth of the prison until a door opened into the air. The light was dim and dusted with small stars. The moon was just about visible behind wispy clouds. There were tall, unmanned towers around the high prison walls. Curls of barbed wire sat atop the walls. The yard was dusty and empty. There was a deathly chill in the air that was both foreboding and oppressive, but still Jay walked out into the yard.

In the middle of the yard, and it was what Luke was heading towards, was a tree. It seemed incongruous with the rest of the prison. The tree had a thick trunk and low branches that fanned out, covered with leaves and fruit. The starlight dripped down onto the tree, making it appear to glisten.

"What is this?" Jay asked when he arrived at the tree. Luke reached up and plucked a piece of fruit from the tree. It was round, shiny and red.

"This would have all been easier if you had just eaten the apple I offered you before," Luke said. "But I suppose you had your process and you wanted to work through things your own way."

"My own way? What the hell are you talking about?" Jay asked.

Luke smirked. "That's quite an appropriate choice of words. Just eat the apple and everything will become clear," he said as he tossed the apple to Jay. Jay caught it. It fit nicely into his palm. He looked it over, but was still confused.

"What is this doing here? And how do you know about it? Who are you really? Am I really the warden? *Answer me!*"

"If you want answers, then you'll have to eat the fruit. It will give you all the knowledge you need. That's why you planted it here in the first place," Luke said.

Jay was still confused. He didn't have any memory of planting the tree. He looked upon the fruit with suspicion, but he knew that Luke wasn't going to give him answers any other way. It might well have been a trick because the longer Jay spent with Luke, the more he got the feeling that he couldn't trust him, but in this instance he had little choice. His memories were elusive, so he didn't have much to lose. He brought the fruit to his lips and sweetness filled his mouth as he bit into it. There was a satisfying crunch. Suddenly, things started coming back to him. He opened his eyes and looked at Luke as the air shimmered around the man. From his back sprouted dark, feathery wings that were tattered and frayed. As soon as Jay saw them, he was quick to anger. He rushed to Luke, dropping the fruit on the ground, and pinned Luke against the tree, lifting Luke's feet off the ground.

"What is this? What have you done to me, Lucifer?" Jay growled.

Amusement flickered upon Lucifer's face.

"Ah, so you do remember me? I'm glad to see it worked. Would you prefer for me to keep calling you Jay or should I use the name you gave yourself?"

"What. Have. You. Done?" Jay growled between gritted teeth.

"I didn't do anything, Jay. You did. I'm only here because you asked me."

Suddenly Jay's mind was filled with more images. He staggered back. Lucifer stretched his neck to ease away the pain.

The hammering. The hammering. The cries of pain. His son… his only son being nailed to a cross and all because He had made it so. Rivers of blood flowed down the body and the wood, dripping on the ground, while the son looked up to the father and asked for a reason for the pain, and the father could only give him one answer…

Because it must be so.

"No, I... How could I do this? Why would I do this?" Jay asked, looking at his palms as though he expected them to be covered in blood. "Why would I ask *you* here?"

"Because despite everything that happened between us, I'm the only one who can understand you. The others are all sycophants. They'll only tell you what you want to hear and, if you ask me, that's one of the reasons why things have gotten so bad. You never have anyone to give you a dissenting opinion," Lucifer sighed. "But I digress. That's not really why we're here. It will come back to you as the fruit does its work, but to expedite matters, I'll fill you in. You wanted to take away your own memory to see if you could figure out what you did wrong without the knowledge that you have accrued over the years. But things started going wrong from the very beginning, really. As soon as you gave them the ability to choose, they were doomed."

"You were the one who tempted them," Jay spat.

Lucifer laughed and shook his head. "You *wanted* me to tempt them. Yes, that's the part that the story forgets. Oh, it was so convenient that you just happened to leave for a little while so that they had to fend for themselves. It's not like it was hard to tempt them anyway. Besides, you were only so angry because it was *your* knowledge in the tree."

Jay waved him away with a dismissive hand.

"But why all the pain?" Jay asked.

"It's a part of life. You can't stop it. That's what you don't understand. Perfection is a lie. That's why you threw me out, because I dared speak out against your idealized vision for life. But it doesn't work. You've tried before. After the flood, you thought that you could begin again and things would be better because you had noble people to carry on your message, but, over time, things went awry. When you gave them literal laws, they found loopholes or they applied them far too strictly. Then, all the messages with plagues..." he shook his head, "the fact is that free will is a flaw to perfection because people are always going to make mistakes. You're never going to be able to change that."

"But I sent them my *son*," Jay choked on the word.

"I know… What better messenger to send than your will made flesh? But, even then, it wasn't that easy. People are fickle. Their natures are such that they're never going to do what you expect them to do. I have to give your boy credit though. I tried my best to tempt him, but he held out. It was actually him that made me think there might be a chance for them after all."

"I killed him… I sent him to his death."

"I know," Lucifer said. "I've always been a bit curious as to why. Has it got something to do with Abraham?"

Jay nodded.

"Ah, I thought that seeing him again might spark something inside you."

"I did it for him," Jay said. "I did it for all of them. I thought if they could see what kind of sacrifice I would be willing to make for them that it might make them better. I had cleansed the world of the impure. I had punished them. I had tried to make them see the error of their ways, but nothing worked. I thought if I could give them my son's life, they would finally see how much I care about them, but it hasn't changed a thing. They still kill. They still fight. They still let their hearts be guided by hatred and envy and all these petty emotions. I just don't understand where I went wrong."

"Some might say that creating them in the first place was the first mistake," Lucifer said, although he quickly changed tack when Jay glared at him. "I think your mistake is in expecting too much of them. They're not like you and I. This world isn't governed by the same rules as our realms. There's more chaos here, but that doesn't have to be a bad thing. They're still capable of surprising us."

"I never wanted this for them. I wanted them to be happy. I wanted them to have a good world," Jay said.

"And you gave them one, but a part of the gift you gave them was the ability to mess it all up. So, now you have to ask yourself what you're going to do. Are you going to take that gift away? Are you going to cleanse the world and try again? Do we have to prepare for another reckoning?"

Jay thought about it for a few moments, then he shook his head. "Actually, I think it might be better if I stay out of things for a while. This all weighs heavily on me... Maybe if I leave them to their own devices, they'll begin to set themselves straight. I should never have interfered in the first place. Perhaps if I had left Adam and Eve alone, things would have been different."

"Perhaps, but then again we would have missed out on a lot of fun along the way. Let's do this again sometime. It's been interesting," Lucifer said as they walked towards the prison gates. Jay remained silent, thinking about the nature of the world he created. His heart was heavy with sorrow for all he had done to try and make things better. He knew he needed to make penance for all he had done, but he also knew he couldn't rid the world of his creation. It was time for him to stop interfering and let them figure things out by themselves.

The 'FU-GO' Legacy

Prologue

An unnamed island in the Pacific Ocean, late 1944, before the end of World War II

Flame warred with water as the boat streaked through the tide. Foamy ripples surged through holes. Steam hissed and crackled as the fire streamed across the deck, tearing through flesh and cloth, dancing wildly as though it was in the middle of a hedonic daze. The boat was teetering to its port side as the crew tried to steady it, even though there was a sinking feeling that all hope was lost. The Japanese boat *Obi* groaned as it was being torn apart by the strain of fighting against its demise. The wounds left from the American torpedoes were great gashes in the hull and although the intrepid and loyal crew had served their duty and sunk the America ship, they feared that the damage sustained was too great.

There were heavy lurching sounds, like a bellowing whale taking its last breaths. The glittering sea churned as the boat rocked from side to side. The electrical equipment crackled and fizzed as the communications officer tried in vain to send a message home, to alert the homeland of their great success and to ensure that their names and their valour were remembered and honoured.

Static was the only reply; as water surged around his waist, he closed his eyes and gave up hope.

The Japanese sailors tried their best to salvage their ship as it was pulled into the watery depths. The shadowy abyss below contrasted with the fire that was spreading across the deck of the ship. Panic spread through the usually stoic crew. Wailing cries peppered the air as some were caught in the flames, while others flung themselves into the sea, hoping that the water would be their salvation.

It wasn't.

Jagged pieces of metal bobbed in the surface, looking like shark fins. Their sharp edges caught flesh and soon enough the water was streaked with blood. Dark shadows bloomed underneath the surface of the water. Sailors flailed their arms about, their deathly wails puncturing the otherwise silent paradise they had found themselves in.

The battle had been a furious one. They had caught the America ship unawares. Stealth had given them the advantage, but the American's had hit back and they had hit hard. The *Obi* had limped away, taking on water all the time. The crew had tried to patch up the vessel, but it was hopeless. Now, there was nothing to do but abandon ship. When the call came, there was a sigh of relief from many of the crew. As much as they knew it was their duty to go down with their ship, a shred of them wanted to cling to life. They left their posts and sprinted towards whatever life rafts remained. Many of them had been damaged too and hung loosely from the ship. There were fights between comrades as they knew there was limited space and, in this instance, when there was such a fine line between life and death there was no time for honour or politeness. They clawed like wild animals and the weaker ones perished.

One by one, the crew abandoned their ship. On the bridge, the captain and the first officer stood resolute, looking out at the glistening sea, that had the sun dancing upon it. The ship shuddered and they were barely able to keep their footing. The first officer, Ishibashi Hideaki, had a red cloth wrapped around his head. Blood seeped out of the tight bandage from a wound that had been sustained in the attack. He was light headed and dazed, trying to drag his captain away from the bridge.

"We must go," he said in a harsh tone, shouting to be heard over the cacophony of destruction that seized the ship. "There is no more time. There is no hope. We must leave *now.*" He grabbed his captain, but the captain shrugged him off. Nishihara Ryu was a strong, determined man. Ishibashi had looked up to him in awe through all the time he had served under him. There was nobody more honourable, nobody more dutiful, but at this moment in time, Ishibashi decided there was nobody more stupid.

"I cannot leave. I must stay with the ship."

"This is no place for tradition! This is your *life* we're talking about. You can't stay here, not when it means certain death. If we have any hope of surviving, we're going to need a leader. We're going to need *you*," Ishibashi said through gritted teeth, glaring at Captain Ryu. The captain's eyes were steel as he remained unmoved, as though he was as much a part of this ship as all the other ramparts and beams and hull plating.

"They have a leader. You. You have served me well, Ishibashi, and you can lead them to survival. My place is here. It is the way it must be. It is our honour."

"Damn our honour!" Ishibashi cried. Captain Ryu hadn't winced when the ship had been attacked. He hadn't winced when they had all realized there was no way they could prevent the water from sinking the boat and he hadn't winced when the fire spread. But he did wince when Ishibashi uttered this sentiment that went against everything Captain Ryu believed in.

"Stop!" Captain Ryu said the word with such force that it slammed through the air.

"If we do not act with honour in the most trying times, then it is worth nothing. This is who we are. This is what it means to be Japanese. Take this lesson with you wherever you end up. Lead the crew. Remind them who we are. Never lose our traditions. Never lose this." As he said this, he turned his arm and pointed to the Japanese flag. Ishibashi was filled with admiration yet again for his captain. There was no finer leader, no finer man, and as much as Ishibashi hated him for staying, he also knew that it couldn't be any other way. If Captain Ryu abandoned his post, then he wouldn't be the man Ishibashi had admired.

"I will do as you ask, but I am not sure I can lead them," Ishibashi admitted, turning his gaze away in shame.

"You can and you will," Captain Ryu said with absolute certainty in his voice. "Because it is an order."

Ishibashi nodded solemnly and knew there was nothing else he could do. The boat lurched wildly once again and almost pulled Ishibashi off his feet, but somehow Captain Ryu remained unmoved. Ishibashi left the bridge and ran through the boat, evading flames, trying not to weep as he saw the limp bodies of his fallen comrades, most of them with anguished looks on their faces, some with their skin so mottled from burns they were unrecognizable. The hollow gaze in their eyes was something he would never forget, not to his dying day.

He sprinted across the deck and made his way to the final life raft, jumping in as it descended from the boat. The oarsmen rowed away from the Obi. Ishibashi held up his eyes to shield himself from the glare of the flames. The air was hot, shimmering with deathly fire, while everyone cried around him in shock and mourning. There were other crewmen who hadn't been as fortunate as the ones in the boat. They were bobbing up and down in the water, crying for assistance as they were caught in the ship's shadow. There was no hope for them now. Ishibashi had to think like a captain and lead his people to safety, however many there were left. The oars crashed through the waves and they got further and further from the ship. The crackling, devastating fire became a faint glow; the cries of the damned became nothing more than whispers in their minds. Dark smoke rose in a thick plume; Ishibashi forced himself to watch it. Sorrow welled in his heart and, although his usual inclination was to push aside emotions like these, especially in war where emotional vulnerability was a weakness, he allowed it to wash over him because it was the least he could do for his fallen comrades.

He thought of his captain going down with the ship, plunging into the watery depths from which there was no escape. No doubt Captain Ryu would have had that same stoic look on his face as he always wore. The unflappable man was incredible and Ishibashi had no idea how he was going to live up to the example set. The boat bobbed along, getting farther and farther away from the wreck with every passing moment until the horizon rose and he set eyes on the *Obi* for the final time, but every face of the crew was etched into his heart and he would follow his orders to the best of his ability.

*

Ishibashi had no idea how much time had passed. Out there, there was nothing apart from the endless sea and the sun beating upon them. His lips were cracked and his muscles ached. Other sailors were hanging over the edge of the boat, while the few who had any energy left were rowing, although at a much slower speed than before. Ishibashi blinked and forced himself to row to set an example to his men, because it's what Captain Ryu would have done. In the distance, he could see a couple of the other boats that had managed to break free of the wreck. They seemed to be heading in the same direction, although where it would lead them he did not know. His orders were to lead his men to safety, but how could he be expected to carry out that order when there was so much unknown? For all he knew, they were in the middle of the ocean and by escaping the *Obi* they had only delayed the inevitable. He didn't let this on to his men though. They exchanged few words. Each of them were dealing with their own personal hell, shaken and tormented by what they had witnessed. Ishibashi had never known a war like this one and the horrors that were contained within it were truly evil. He just hoped that his empire would emerge triumphant and spread order across the world. It was the only thing that would make the sacrifice of his men worthwhile. His men... They were *his* now.

Suddenly, Ishibashi barked orders to rouse the other sailors. He clapped his hands and urged them to recover their strength. They moaned at first, but eventually their momentum increased and the oars surged through the waves again. Ishibashi stopped looking behind him to look ahead. He watched the horizon, hoping against hope that something would appear, something that would break up the endless, eternal horizon.

When it finally did, he could barely believe it. His lips parted and he gasped. He strained his eyes to check that he wasn't hallucinating, for he knew that being out in the ocean like this could do strange things to a man's mind, even one as disciplined as his. But then another member of his crew shouted in triumph and he knew that if they were seeing the same thing, then it really existed. A land mass appeared, growing bigger and bigger all the time, offering hope and salvation and a step towards the future.

Three ships descended upon the island and once they reached land, the crew staggered out onto the sandy shore, falling to their knees and praying in thanks to whichever god had offered them salvation. They ran to the tree line and foraged for fruit and berries, not caring if they were poisonous or not. One of them found a stream of fresh water and they all slaked their thirst, greedily gulping down as much water as they could. As the sun set and a shadow fell across the land, the temperature cooled. The water lapped gently against the shore, as though it was the most benign thing in the world. Ishibashi knew better though. It could be a harsh mistress and it had already pulled many of his countrymen into its embrace. But he and the other men were still standing, still carrying the honour of their country in their hearts.

While other men foraged for food or just lay in the sand, shocked and traumatised by what had occurred, Ishibashi found a large stick and cut off a portion of his shirt, forming a makeshift flag. He gathered all his men around and held the flag up high, before plunging it into the sand, so deep that it stood up without him having to support it.

"We come to this land as survivors. We lost a lot today, but we have not lost our lives. We have not lost our dignity. We have not lost our honour. It is important that we continue our traditions and the ways of our people. No matter what happens, we are still Japanese soldiers and we will fight this war until we die. This is now a Japanese outpost. As long as we stand tall, no matter what happens in the rest of the world, Japan still lives on."

His words were met with cheers as the men looked at each other, galvanised by the patriotic spirit. Ishibashi gazed at the flag that fluttered in the wind and prayed that he could make Captain Ryu proud. It might be a long time until they were rescued, but it was his order to survive.

Chapter One

Decades later…

"And nobody ever came for us?" Nagasawa asked, his young eyes blinking as he tilted his head towards his father. Ishibashi was an old man by now, but his son was young and both generations were bound by loyalty to the old ways. They sat on the beach in front of the flag that was caught by a gentle breeze. The material was the same as Ishibashi had used on that fateful day when they had washed up on this island, which the natives called Okka. The flag was faded and sun bleached now, but the image was a powerful one and they waited on the shore for someone to come for them.

It had been many years since Ishibashi had landed on the island. After taming the surrounding area, they had explored the island and found a native tribe. Some of the Japanese men were quick to mingle with the natives, while others were slow to forget the country they had come from and those they had left behind. The natives were friendly

293

and, after some trading, they had come to good terms with the Japanese and basically divided the island between themselves, although there was much movement between the villages to make the population almost indistinguishable from each other.

"Nobody ever did," Ishibashi said, tears glistening in his eyes. He looked wistfully out to sea. "And I don't know why. I always thought they would. Every morning and every night, I used come out here just in case someone came for us or in case a plane flew over, but there has been nothing. Sometimes I worry that we are the last Japanese people left in the world. That is why we must remain loyal to our traditions. If we forget who we are, then we forget all of Japan."

"I will not forget, father. I will remember the stories and the ways, and I will make sure others listen."

Ishibashi smiled. "You are a good son, Nagasawa. Your heart is Japanese, even though you have not set foot on our homeland. You remind me of Captain Ryu."

Nagasawa bowed his head as he accepted the compliment. He knew that there was nobody his father thought more highly of. "Your honour me with your words," he said.

"I wish that you could have met him. But it was not his place to be here."

"I'm sure he would have been proud of you," Nagasawa said.

"I hope so," Ishibashi replied, continuing to gaze at the flag. "I hope so."

He groaned as he stood. Nagasawa nimbly leapt to his feet and helped his old man up. Ishibashi sighed at how his body was failing him. Time seemed to flow differently here in this quiet, remote part of the world, but he was still succumbing to the same rigors that plagued everybody. There was always a new ache somewhere around his body; it was only a matter of time until it failed completely, but at least he knew the future of his little Japanese colony was in good hands. It had taken him a long time to bring a child into the world, but he looked at Nagasawa with pride.

"May I go and play with the others before it is time to sleep?" Nagasawa asked.

"You may," Ishibashi allowed, nodding his head. He smirked as Nagasawa sprinted along the beach, kicking up sand as he went. He sighed. Was he ever that young?

He returned along the path through the trees towards the small village that had been built up over the years. Small fires glowed, providing warmth and illumination for the people inside. He opened his door and smiled at his wife. The young woman was pretty. Her skin was a shade of midnight and her hair was long and thick. Her body was shapely, her eyes wide and bright. Her name was Suna and she was devoted to him. It had been a great honour for her to marry the leader of the Japanese and much pride was bestowed upon her family, but to Ishibashi she was so young that it was hard to love her in a romantic way. It didn't help that his heart belonged to someone else.

Suna smiled at him and brought him over some tea, bowing her head as she did so, as he had taught her. He took the rudimentary cup and smiled gratefully, sipping the refreshing tea.

"Where is Nagasawa?" she asked.

"Playing with his friends," Ishibashi said. Suna's voice was soft and her words were broken, but she had shown remarkable progress in learning Japanese. It was such a shame, he thought, that her love was wasted on a man like him. "I told him it would be alright just this once. I was telling him about the old days again. It makes me think-"

"Of her?" Suna asked. There was a slight edge to her voice. Ishibashi turned away in shame. Suna had always been understanding, but it was natural for her to be a little jealous, even of a ghost.

Ishibashi nodded, an almost imperceptible gesture, but one that spoke volumes to Suna. "Still? Even now?"

"Always," Ishibashi said in a trembling voice, choking on emotion. Tears welled up in his eyes. "And I am sorry for that. I wish things could be different. I wish I could be the kind of man you deserve."

Suna placed her hand on his shoulder and squeezed it. "And I wish you liked this life as much as I did. You always claim this to be your home, but I see you watching the shore every day waiting for someone to come, even after all this time. Your heart has never truly been here. Everything you've done here has been of necessity, even having a son."

"That may be true, but I am glad I did. I regret that I took so long to father a child. Nagasawa is everything a father could want in a son and he will be a good successor to me when it is my time to leave."

"Do not speak of such things," Suna withdrew her hand and her face was stricken with panic. "You tempt the spirits. If they hear you whisper about death, they will come and take you away. You are still a strong man. You still have much life left in you yet."

Ishibashi wished that he shared her optimism. He could feel himself getting older. As much as this island was invigorating, he knew the effects would not last forever, but at least he had kept to his order. At least he had made sure that his crew survived.

He finished his tea and went to bed, while Suna stayed up for a while. There was a small part of the bedroom that was devoted to his past. His old shirt was hung up, tattered and stained now. He slipped his fingers into the pocket and pulled out an old picture. It was creased and had almost faded completely in time, but the image could still be made out, the image of his Keiko. He closed his eyes as he did every night and was transported back to a time before the war, when he was walking through a sun-drenched meadow with the most beautiful young woman he had ever seen. When he looked in her eyes and drowned in her heavenly smile, he saw his future unfold before him and it was glorious. They spoke of children and marriage and all the places they wanted to see. She loved him as much as he loved her, but he could never understand how she could feel that way about him.

Then, the war started. She understood that Ishibashi had to do his duty. He promised that he would return one day, that they would have the future they had promised each other, but then he had been stranded on this island. He often wondered what had happened to her. He had always assumed that he would find out one day, but now that possibility was growing less and less likely.

He had promised his heart to Keiko a long time ago and, as such, he had never been able to give all of himself to Suna. He had resisted, wanting to be loyal to the promise he had made so long ago, even though Keiko likely thought he was dead, but as time grew on Ishibashi realized he needed to do something. He was getting older and he could not leave this life without having a child, someone to carry on his legacy. Thus, Nagasawa was born.

*

Nagasawa ran through the woods with a grin on his face. He was in pursuit of Hana, a girl who made him feel intoxicated whenever he was around her. They had a similar complexion, a blending of the Japanese shade and that of the native people. Nagasawa, like his father, was stoic and reserved, but Hana was the complete opposite. She had inherited more from the native people on the island than from the Japanese settlers. She was an explorer, bold and brave, and never had any fear; Nagasawa was utterly and completely besotted with her.

"I'm going to get you!" he yelled as he burst through a thicket of trees and then stopped abruptly, looking around because he was sure that he would have found her here. There was a blank look on his face as he peered through the dim light to try and find her. He could hear her giggle drifting through the air and strained his ears, trying to pinpoint the origin. He assumed she was behind a tree, so he crept up to the nearest one and pounced, but there was nothing there. He pouted and frowned, glancing around in confusion.

"I'm up here," a light, lilting voice said. Nagasawa stepped back and tilted his head up, looking into the branches. Hana was sitting on a long, thick branch, her legs dangling down. Her thick black hair framed her face and her smile was wide.

"That's not fair!" Nagasawa protested, but Hana just laughed.

"Are you going to come up here to join me or what?" she asked.

Nagasawa pressed his lips together as he never usually liked climbing trees, but he placed his feet in the crook of the trunk and pulled himself up. Hana stood up too and pointed up higher, indicating that she wanted to ascend the tree. She was off before Nagasawa had even reached the first branch, but although he found her tiring and troublesome, there was a flicker of excitement inside as well. They eventually ended up on a tall branch. From this vantage point, they could see to the farthest point of the island and gaze into the ocean all around them. This was their whole world and it was beautiful, but to Nagasawa, Hana was the most beautiful of all. The stars flanked the moon in a glittering dance and the night was peaceful.

"I saw you with your father again," Hana said. "Does he still think people are going to come and find him?"

"I think it's become more of a tradition now than anything else."

Hana snorted a laugh. "Your father and traditions."

"Traditions are important. They teach us about who we are, about our culture and how we should behave," Nagasawa said indignantly.

"I think it restricts people. We should be able to behave how we want," Hana said.

"If we do that, then we lose something special about ourselves," Nagasawa replied. "We are Japanese even if we are far from the home of our ancestors. That means something. It's important to take these lessons to heart and pass them on to our children. Many men died in the war my father fought. They died to preserve our way of life and our traditions. We cannot let them die in vain."

"Would you fight if the war came to us?"

"Yes," Nagasawa said without any hesitation.

"Then I suppose I would have to fight too. Someone would have to make sure that you didn't die," Hana leaned into him, nudging him.

Nagasawa grinned. "Then we would protect each other."

"That is the way. Especially if we are to be married," she said, a sparkle illuminating her eyes. Nagasawa's eyes widened in shock, for he believed that he had kept his emotions hidden. The path of love had been a treacherous one to walk and it had not been easy to understand what was happening behind Hana's eyes.

"Married?"

"It is what you want, yes?" she asked.

Nagasawa swallowed a lump in his throat and licked his lips. "Well, yes... I suppose it is, eventually. But how did you know?"

Hana laughed in that effortless way of hers, as though the whole world was a joke. "I've known forever!" she exclaimed and lowered her voice as she leaned into him. "And I've known because I want it too. I have already spoken with my father about it. He would like to have words with you," she said.

"I'm sure that can be arranged," Nagasawa said.

Hana laughed again. "You have just been told that the woman you love wants to marry you and still you sit there like a stone. Oh, Nagasawa, you do make me laugh," she said as she flung her arms around him and nestled into the crook of his neck. Nagasawa breathed in the sweet scent that flooded him and felt himself tingle all over. The soft form of her body pressed against him and he suddenly felt more alive than he ever had before. He turned his head to look at her directly and lost himself in her eyes. They had never kissed before, but in his mind, they had kissed a thousand times at least, yet none of those could compare to the real thing. A smile twitched on his lips as they seemed to be drawn together by an invisible force. He sensed her warm breath first and suddenly the world opened up to him; he realized that he had never lived at all. The kiss was warm and sweet, but just as he was surrendering to the bliss, there was a loud noise that shook his attention. He and Hana both turned and looked in horror at the bright orange blaze that took hold of the opposite end of the forest, the end where the natives lived, the end where Hana's family lived.

"No..." she gasped as she scrambled down the tree. Nagasawa followed her. There were cries of anguish as others became aware of what was happening. They ran towards the other village, but they did not make it there in time. The air was thick with smoke and the ground was scorched. Nagasawa had never seen anything like it. Hana dropped to her knees and wept along with the others. He turned to see Ishibashi standing there.

"Father… What is this?" Nagasawa asked.

"I'm not sure, son, but I believe the war has finally come back to us."

Chapter Two

A research station in the USA

Miranda Cho was a slim woman who swept her dark hair up in a tangled mess upon her head and wore slim glasses. Currently, she was hunched over a map of the world with lines running all over it that signified the air currents. Her face was pinched as she looked up and gazed at the pictures that adorned her wall, pictures of forest fires that had occurred all over the United States and the islands in the Pacific Ocean. She shook her head and groaned at the devastation. There were a number of theories floating around. Some saw it as a direct attack on American soil that deserved immediate retaliation, although thankfully these incendiary thoughts were not shared by those who actually had the power to make decisions. Another theory was that the climate had changed so drastically fires could spark into life with little to no cause. But there was another theory, one that had been called outlandish at first, but which Miranda thought was more and more likely the more these fires started happening.

At first, there seemed to be no pattern to these fires. They appeared randomly, as though they had been an act of God, but Miranda had never been a religious person. She wasn't willing to ascribe faith to something that could be explained by science. There was an explanation for everything; she just had to be patient enough to find it. It had taken hours of her looking at the data again and again, but she thought she had finally cracked it.

"Ben, come in here!" she yelled. Ben, her husky colleague, walked in looking the worse for wear. Both of them were overworked and underpaid, but he showed the effects more than she did.

"I was just about to come in. There's something you should know," he began.

"That can wait. I think I've finally been proved right. Look at the pattern of these air currents," she said excitedly, gesturing to the open map that had been spread out before her. "If you look at the way these jet streams flow, it fits, Ben. They all pass over where these fires started. And if we trace them back, look where they lead," she dragged her fingers across the jet streams to Japan. "It has to be the Fu Go bombs. It's the only thing that makes sense."

"I'm not sure that's true..." Ben said.

"It is! Come on, nobody knew where these Fu Go bombs went during the war. Sure, plenty of them might have just fallen into the ocean somewhere along the way, but what if they didn't? What if all this time they've been floating around the world and only now they're starting to do what they're designed to do?"

"Why wouldn't they have exploded before now?"

Miranda shrugged. "I guess they weren't designed that well. I mean, they were just balloon bombs. But if this is true, then we have a cause, and we can scan the air for more to prevent it from happening again."

"That's what I came to talk to you about," Ben said. "I just got word that there has been another fire, this time on a small island in the Pacific Ocean. I guess we can definitely rule out the theory that it's a direct attack on America."

"Or, if I'm right, it's an attack that has just taken decades to actually happen. Let's get out there. Maybe we can find information to confirm my theory." Her eyes were wild with excitement at the prospect of discovering something new about the world. If she could learn what actually caused these fires, then she could prevent them from happening again.

"It's strange, isn't it, to think that something from that long ago can still be floating around out there. I know these balloon bombs can't think, but it's almost as though they believe the war is still going on."

Chapter Three

Ishibashi had never seen anything like it since the day he had first arrived on the island. The air glowed through the smoke, dangerous and blazing. He coughed and stepped back as the thick smoke whispered through the forest. Sweat prickled his brow; when he breathed in, he could smell bitter ash and burnt flesh. When he closed his eyes, he remembered how he had ran through the *Obi* and seen so many men, lifeless and limp.

The settlers had acted quickly, bringing great buckets of water to put out the fire. They managed to stop it from spreading to the rest of the island, but they were too late to save their brethren. Some of the natives had managed to flee the blaze. They pointed to the sky and said that something had come from the heavens to spread fire. Ishibashi had a sick feeling in his stomach. He directed the relief effort and walked through the ashy remains of the village as the dead were brought out and laid in a pile. There were too many, far too many. He thought he had put this all behind him, but it seemed as though the war was not quite done with him yet.

The night had been a peaceful one, but this blaze had torn through the island so quickly it had changed the course of their destiny. The mood was sombre and many tears were shed. In the depths of the night, Ishibashi gathered his people and the natives together.

"We cannot bring back those who died tonight. This tragedy is something that I would not wish upon my worst enemies, but it appears our enemies do not wish the same. Some of you, like me, remember the war. Others know it through stories. For a long time now, I believed that we left this war behind, but it seems as though it has found us again. This attack has been so devastating that I can only believe it has come from our enemies. The war is arriving and we have prepared for it. We have trained well and we know how to defend our home. I will not let this island fall into the hands of the Americans. I will not lose this war after all this time. Those of you who are capable of fighting, gather at my village and we will prepare our defences. Those of you who are not, take care of the dead. We shall honour them by surviving."

Ishibashi's words were clear through the still night and they galvanised the spirit of those around him, but deep inside he was filled with dread. Although his life hadn't been perfect, it had been peaceful. The days had been free of conflict and he had been able to put the horror of war behind him, but with this attack, it was as though he was thrust directly back into conflict again. He might as well have been a young man, standing in the bridge beside his captain as the ship was attacked, surrounded by fire and flame. His hands trembled and his throat was dry. All he wished was that he could survive for a little longer.

Nagasawa caught up with him as they returned to their village. Hana was tending to the destroyed village, likely searching for her parents.

"Are you certain it is the enemy?" Nagasawa asked.

"What else could it be?" Ishibashi replied. Nagasawa had no answer for him.

"But why would they attack after all this time? How could the war still be continuing after all these years?"

"I do not know. I thought by now it would have been over. If it has been going on for this long, then it is the bloodiest war that has ever existed. I can only hope that our people have been able to hold on for this long. But if the enemy has reached us, then perhaps they seek to destroy the last Japanese outpost. Perhaps they have scoured the seas for us to track down any survivor."

"Would they really do that?"

"They were bloodthirsty then. I cannot imagine what decades of war has done to them. I'm sure they're more like beasts than men. It is a horrible thing to imagine. I cannot believe that the world has ended up like this. It was never supposed to be this way. The war was supposed to have an end."

"I wonder what happened. Perhaps this isn't the same war. Perhaps it's a different one."

"Wars are all the same. There are just different reasons."

"And now we have to fight."

314

"Yes, we must."

"What if we die?"

"Then we die, but as long as we die with honour, we can be proud to say that we are Japanese."

"I do not want to die with honour, father. I don't want to die at all. I have only just begun to live," Nagasawa said. When Ishibashi looked at his son, he saw something that had been etched upon his own face many years ago – the first bloom of love. Ishibashi had always assumed that his son would have been spared the same tragedy that had befallen him, but perhaps life was just a cycle; patterns were doomed to echo and repeat throughout the years.

"As long as we fight well, we shall be able to repel the invaders," Ishibashi said, although he wished he was as confident as he sounded.

*

Warriors, old and young, gathered on the beach. They held their weapons proudly. Ishibashi had his pistol in his hand. It was a weapon he hadn't picked up since he had first arrived on the island for there was no way to replace the bullets once they had been fired. Others had rifles they had salvaged from the boat, although there were only a few of these as there hadn't been enough time to gather a good supply from the *Obi*. The other weapons were more primitive – spears and bows and arrows. Kensei swords had been formed as well, a perfect marriage between the Japanese ingenuity and the natural resources that the natives could harvest. Ishibashi spoke to them.

"The enemy is dangerous. The enemy is fierce. It has been a long time since we have fought them, but I have no doubt they are the same as they were then. They are thirsty for blood and they will fight until there is nothing left in them. Years ago, we were stranded here because of an attack that had hit us after we thought the enemy had been defeated. Do not assume that you are safe. As long as they have breath left in their body, they will fight and they will seek to take away what we have built here. I do not know why they have chosen to come here and attack us after all this time. It is a symbol of how ruthless they are and I can only imagine that they have managed to gain the upper hand in the war. It is quite possible that the Japan we know and love has been destroyed. We may be all that is left of our people, so we must fight as ruthlessly as them. We know this island. We are masters of this terrain and, although their weapons may be mightier than ours, I am sure that we can triumph. We must be patient, strike when they least expect it and blend in with the shadows. It is going to be difficult. Many of us will lose our lives, but you must remember that we die for each other. As long as some of us survive, all of us survive. Go now and prepare for battle. The enemy may appear at any time."

Ishibashi surprised himself with how easily he slipped into the role of a soldier again. When he had first joined the army it had felt as though he was wearing a costume and playing a part in a theatre production. That was until he faced his first battle and killed his first man. The reality had set in quickly. That aspect of his life had been pushed aside ever since he had arrived on the island, but he had never been able to forget it. It was strange, really; he had almost forgotten what he wanted to be before he joined the army. It seemed as though destiny had labelled him a soldier.

He was older now and he knew his chances of surviving were slim. Nerves jangled in his heart like an old clanging bell as he waited and waited for the enemy to appear. He couldn't believe that they would just drop a bomb like that and leave the island to burn. It must have been a way to unsettle them before the attack. He had to be vigilant.

He thought of Suna and how he had not been as good a husband to her as he should have been. He thought of Nagasawa and how he had been too old to be a proper father. There were so many things he would have done differently if he had the choice, but it was too late now to make any difference. He wondered if Captain Ryu had experienced the same fleeting thoughts as the *Obi* had been embraced by the sea. The mood on the island was thick with tension and Ishibashi's heart thundered in his chest, knowing that death was coming for him. He had to delay it as much as possible.

*

"I thought you would have stayed with the others," Nagasawa said as Hana crept up to him. She wasn't wearing her usual smile. Something about her seemed more lifeless than usual, which was understandable given the circumstances. Nagasawa wasn't himself either. He had never seen anything like this. Although he had heard horrible stories from his father and the other old soldiers, seeing something like that in real time was indescribable. There was a nauseous feeling settling in the pit of his stomach and he wasn't sure it would ever go away. He held onto his bow and arrow as though they offered him life, and he was glad that Hana had come to join him.

"I did all I could. Staying there would have only meant I'd be wallowing in my thoughts and I didn't want that. I wanted to do something productive. At least if I'm here I can distract myself."

"Are you sure a distraction is what you need? It might help to talk about it."

"No," Hana said bluntly. "I just want to forget for a while," she said, although she had the kind of look in her eyes that told Nagasawa she would never forget this. He nodded anyway.

"I'm sorry I missed your father's speech," she said.

"It was a good one, although I have to admit it chilled me. I never thought the war would come for us. The way father spoke about the rest of the world sounded so far away and distant. I thought we were separate from all that."

"I did too, but if the enemy is as bad as your father says, then it is no surprise that they have found us. At least we have trained for this day."

"Yes, although I'm not sure the training ever prepared me for the way I feel, how scared I am," Nagasawa's voice was even, but inside his emotions were churning violently. They were eased when Hana slipped her hand across his and clasped it tightly.

"As long as we are together, nobody can defeat us," she said. He wasn't sure if she meant the two of them specifically, or the Japanese and natives working together, but either way, it was a comforting thing to say.

"It happened at the worst time," Nagasawa said, eyeing her sheepishly. Despite everything, the kiss was still on his mind, as well as everything it promised. For a moment, the sorrow fled from Hana's face and she smiled.

"That doesn't change what the future holds. We will make it through this, Nagasawa. I will not see everything taken away from me. We deserve to be together. We deserve happiness. We will make it through this and we will have everything we want. There is nobody I want to be with other than you. There is no future I want other than one with you in it," she said, pressing her forehead to Nagasawa's.

Nagasawa thought that he was going to burst with emotion. He didn't think it was possible to feel this intensely about anyone; yet, his heart was filled with love. It was a deep ache that took a hold of him. They stayed there, together, waiting for the enemy to arrive, hoping that they wouldn't have to break the promise they had made to each other. Nagasawa had never feared his life being taken away from him, but now that he had so much to live for, he knew that he was willing to kill for it.

Chapter Four

Ishibashi had not seen a ship since the *Obi* had disappeared over the horizon. For so long, he had dreamed of one approaching the island with a glistening hull and the promise of being taken home. He had always imagined he would feel utter joy at the sight of a ship, but instead, he was filled with dread. The white hull was bright. The design was not familiar to him, but that didn't surprise him considering how much things must have changed in his absence, at least in the ways of technology. Other things remained the same, like the way of war.

When he saw the boat, it was as though all his worst fears had come true. He hadn't wanted to be proven right about the attack, but it was clear that they were coming. Somehow they had discovered his settlement and they were here to wipe out the last remaining vestige of Japanese culture. Well, they might try, but they would fail. Ishibashi was not going to let this place fall easily.

He put his hands to his mouth and let out a warning cry for the others to prepare themselves. They were arranged, hidden in the trees and behind rocks, waiting to strike once they saw what the enemy had in store for them.

The boat looked huge as it approached. It flew no flag and Ishibashi wondered if the makeup of the global alliances had shifted. There may not have been a Japan, but there might not have been an America either. Such a thing he could only hope for. Adrenaline began to rush through his body and he felt the old instincts kick in. The boat approached the shore, carrying with it inexorable dread. Ishibashi took one last glance around the island, wondering how many of his people were going to survive the attack, wondering how many people he had said his final goodbyes to. He thought of his son and hoped that Nagasawa made it through this. He had a bright future ahead of him and it wasn't fair that it might be cut short.

Then, he thought of Keiko and the life he had left behind. So much time had been spent pondering the different possibilities of life that he perhaps hadn't spent as much time as he should have on the life that had been given to him. There had always been a part of his heart that thought he would see Keiko again, but now he was almost certain that he wouldn't.

The boat continued its approach and then stopped short of the island. Smaller boats descended, filled with men – enemies, soldiers. Ishibashi closed his eyes and found the part of him that was taut and angry, the part of him that was as strong as steel. The enemy had come this far, but their journey was going to end here. As soon as the first of them landed on the beach, they were met with a hail of arrows and javelins. There were cries of triumph as the weapons came flying out and the enemies dropped dead. Ishibashi waited in silence. He and the others with guns were held in reserve for their bullets were precious and they needed to make them count. The enemy was scattered and seemed panicked. Ishibashi smiled. They had probably been expecting a depleted, weak force, but he would show them how strong they were. He had trained his people well and wasn't going to let anyone get the better of them. Bodies fell to the sand and crimson blood seeped out in a pool, staining the white sand before the water lapped it away. The enemy screamed in horror. They had flooded onto the shore, but now they returned to the boat just as quickly, fleeing in panic. Ishibashi smirked. He rose and took aim with his gun, wanting to make his mark on the battle in honour of all the men who had died, including Captain Ryu. His shot cracked through the air and one enemy fell to the ground, his limbs splayed out helplessly. The water dragged those nearest the sea back into the ocean, while the others were left on the shore, a grim reminder that life could end so easily.

Ishibashi and the others walked to the treeline, gazing out at the fleeing enemy who retreated on their rafts to the impressive boat. Ishibashi narrowed his eyes, wondering what had been going through their minds. This was not the enemy he remembered. These did not seem as ruthless as before or as willing to lay down their lives. He had expected them to flood forward, climbing over their dead brethren or even using them as shields. The enemy had little respect for life after all. Instead, they had run away. Perhaps they were not as strong as he believed. Perhaps, instead of a sweeping conquest of the farthest parts of the world, this was more a flailing last strike to accomplish anything. He watched as they retreated to their boat. To his dismay, it did not sail away. Instead, it stayed there, waiting and watching for something to happen. Was there some terrible weapon contained within that would destroy them all? Ishibashi did not know, but he waited for the enemy to make their next move. There was no doubt that they had found more than they had bargained for on the island. Hopefully, they would soon realize that it wasn't worth the time and energy it was going to take to conquer this last proud outpost of the Japanese world.

Chapter Five

The journey across the sea had been relatively calm. Miranda had been examining her data; the more she looked at it, the more she was convinced that she was right. It seemed amazing that a relic could cause this much destruction so long after it had been sent out to wreak havoc, but stranger things had happened. The ship they were on carried a decent-sized crew that also contained a complement of people who were trained in the art of diplomacy, just in case there was some forgotten tribe on the island. It amazed her that there were still parts of the world that had not been explored properly. It was easy to become jaded in this day and age where so much information was available at the touch of a finger and everything already seemed as though it had been discovered, but this showed that there was still some mystery and intrigue left in the world. Miranda was as giddy as she had been as a child, when everything was still new to her.

But that excitement quickly vanished. It was procedure for her to stay behind on the boat in case they met any hostility, which she thought was a stupid precaution to take as she wanted to get out there as quickly as possible, but she obeyed the rules and waited patiently.

She was glad she did.

As soon as her colleagues stepped upon the shore, they were fired upon. Arrows and javelins burst out of the trees and she witnessed men falling before her. Her mouth dropped open and she couldn't turn away even though she wanted to. This act of horror was worse than anything she had seen before. One by one, they fell and blood spread across the beach, staining it with death. Others turned and flailed, but collapsed face first in the water as they were hit in the back, arrows protruding from their bodies. They quickly returned to the ship, but it wasn't quick enough.

Then, something surprising happened, a gunshot rang out.

*

"What the hell is happening out there? Do we have any visuals on the hostiles?" a man called Jack Bull barked out. He was panting and held a bleeding arm. He was one of the lucky ones who had made it back unharmed. Chaos reigned on the boat as the men were pulled up on deck. Everyone ducked for cover, although the hostiles on the island didn't seem to be interested in continuing their attack against the main boat. It was logical to assume they simply didn't want anyone trespassing on their island and they remained well hidden.

"I heard a gunshot," Miranda said. Jack scowled while all the deep creases on his face turned into great valleys and crevices.

"That's not possible. How could they have got their hands on guns?"

"I don't know," Miranda replied.

"Christ, we come here to help them and they treat us like this," Jack winced in pain and punctuated his words with a curse. Miranda licked her lips and brushed an errant strand of hair behind her ear.

"Perhaps they think we're responsible for the fire. Perhaps they think it was a prelude to an invasion."

"I don't care what they think. They just killed my men," Jack said.

Miranda sighed. This certainly wasn't unfolding as she had expected. Usually, when primitive tribes were approached, they acted with caution and curiosity when faced with something they did not understand. It was rare that they should enact such an immediate show of violence. Miranda couldn't get the gunshot out of her mind either. Was it possible that she had misunderstood it as something else? There had certainly been many noises, but a gunshot was a particularly notable sound, especially out here.

She walked across deck, deftly moving between the wounded who had all been brought back. She picked up some binoculars and gazed at the shore, trying to peer beyond the treeline to get a glimpse of the inhabitants of the island. She could see nothing but shadow and an odd hint of movement, but nothing that indicated what type of people these were. As she scanned the shore though, something caught her attention. She adjusted her vision. The island jerked and blurred as she swam across the magnified parts of it. She gasped when she looked at the makeshift flag fluttering in the wind.

"You need to see this," she said, handing the binoculars to Jack. He took them begrudgingly and allowed Miranda to guide her gaze towards what she had seen. At first, he thought she was wasting his time, but then he realized what he was looking at.

"My God..." he said. "How is this possible?"

Miranda didn't have an answer, but she was going to find one. She summoned as much courage as she could before as she walked across the deck and got in a boat. Others were telling her that I was a bad idea, that she should stay while they figured out a plan to deal with the natives, but Miranda didn't think these people were natives at all. If she was right, then she had just discovered something even more remarkable than the cause of forest fires.

Chapter Six

Ishibashi watched the boat carefully. He saw something shimmer near the deck and suspected that whoever was on board was watching them carefully. He smirked to himself, almost goading them to attack again so that they could be driven back again. The enemies must truly have been arrogant to think they could have taken his outpost with such a small force. Perhaps they wouldn't have to fight to the last man after all.

They still had to remain patient. He heard movement nearby. There were whispers and murmurs. He knew the younger generation would be anxious. As much as he had trained them for this, they had never been in this situation before. It was wholly new to them. He remembered the way he had felt overwhelmed the first time he had been in battle, how his hands had trembled and his thoughts whirled inside him at the speed of a tornado. He let out a low animal cry of his own, reminding them to be disciplined and patient. Recklessness now could cost them everything.

Moments later, something happened. Another boat zipped across the shore, away from the main ship. Ishibashi readied himself for another fight, but to his surprise, he could only see one person on the boat, a woman. He furrowed his brow, wondering why a woman would be in a war situation.

As she approached, she held up her hands to show that she was unarmed. Then she yelled in a loud voice. To Ishibashi's surprise, she spoke Japanese and his heart was lifted. Perhaps he had been wrong all this time. Perhaps Japan had won the war!

"I don't know who you are, but we mean you no harm. My name is Miranda Cho and I am here on a scientific expedition. Please don't attack me. We are not here to attack you. We are here to help. Do you have a representative I can speak to?"

She waited patiently. Ishibashi wondered if this was a trap. Perhaps she was sent here to keep them off guard and make them believe that everything was fine. He could almost imagine a hail of gunfire peppering the beach as soon as they stepped out to talk with her. Ishibashi let out a low whistle, indicating for the others to remain hidden. But he was curious about this woman and the information she could offer him. Perhaps she could tell him what had happened in the world during his time on the island. And if it was a trap, then at least the others would be able to retaliate.

The woman stiffened as Ishibashi emerged from the forest. He held his gun pointed at her, for he wanted her to know that she was not going to trick him. The sand was soft under his feet. He walked to the middle of the beach and then waited. Miranda stepped out of her boat and stood on the part of the beach where the water met the sand.

"Who are you?" Ishibashi barked.

Miranda repeated her name and her intentions, and followed up by asking him who he was.

"My name is Ishibashi Hideaki, former first officer of the Japanese destroyer *Obi*. This is our island. You have no place here."

"Believe me, I'm not here to take your place. I just want to help." Miranda spoke in a slow voice and she continued to hold her palms aloft, making it clear that she had no weapon and wasn't reaching for one.

"Are you Japanese?" he asked.

"My parents were Korean. I'm American," she said.

Ishibashi stiffened when she said this and made a show of pointing the gun more directly at her. "You *are* the enemy."

"No," she said quickly, a look of urgency upon her face. "There is no enemy anymore. I think...I think that we need to have a long conversation. Do you still believe a war is happening?"

"Of course. We were just attacked."

"No, that was no attack. It was an accident. It was..." she sighed in frustration. "It's going to take a lot of explaining, but the war ended a long time ago. You've missed out on a lot of history."

Ishibashi wasn't sure that he believed her. It seemed incredulous that the great empire could be undone by the Americans, but she seemed to be sincere.

"How can I believe you? This could be a lie," he said.

"I'm not lying. I promise," she said, putting her hand to her heart. "I know that this must be difficult for you to believe, but I had no idea you were here. There was a fire here, yes?" she asked. Ishibashi nodded. "There have been other fires where I'm from as well. I think I've figured out what's causing them, but I need your help. I can help you too. I can tell you what happened. I can fill you in on everything you've missed and, if you don't believe me, I can prove to you that things have changed."

Ishibashi was still sceptical, but if she could prove it...

"How will you prove this?"

"I have equipment on my boat. If you like, I can take you onto the ship and you can see for yourself, or I can bring it here."

"Bring it here," Ishibashi said, for he wasn't such a fool that he would agree to go into enemy territory.

Miranda nodded and signalled to the ship. Another boat was dropped and with it came a man carrying a blocky black device. Miranda walked up the beach and ushered Ishibashi to come to her. She sat down and unfolded the device. Ishibashi approached cautiously, although he was curious about this thing she had. There was an image before her. She tapped keys and different images flashed upon the screen.

"This might be pretty difficult for you to believe, but this is called a computer. We use it to access an information-sharing service that we call the Internet. It's a way for everyone in the world to share information and communicate with each other. Look," she pulled up a page that was titled *World War II*. He scanned the images and while he couldn't understand most of the words, he recognized the English words for America and Allies."

"America won?" he asked in disbelief, feeling shaken to the core.

"Yes, they did, but it was for the best."

"My country... Is it occupied? Have my people been conquered?" Ishibashi asked in a panicked voice. Miranda smiled and shook her head.

"No, not at all. Once the war ended, Japan was left to rebuild."

"But how did America beat us? We had everything planned. We were winning."

A shadow fell across Miranda's face. "They developed a device called a nuclear bomb. They devastated Hiroshima and Nagasaki. It was not a proud moment for the world, but it did act as a wake-up call. When it was clear that so much power could be controlled, world leaders decided that wars were too risky. Uneasy alliances were made and we have entered a new period of progress. There is still a long way to go, but we have made huge leaps in progression in technology, like this here. I know this must be a shock. I wish I knew how it make it easier for you, but I can only give you the truth."

Ishibashi nodded.

"Did you say your ship was called the *Obi*?" she asked. Ishibashi nodded again. She typed onto the computer once more and a different image flashed onto the screen. He recognized it instantly as the ship. As she scrolled down there were other images, including one of Captain Ryu. Ishibashi let out a soft moan as he saw his old captain, captured here in the prime of his life.

"It says here that the *Obi* was lost at sea. They assumed that all hands were lost." She scrolled down a little farther and then Ishibashi saw a sight that haunted him, his own picture among those of the deceased.

"That's me," he said, pointing to the image on the screen. He could barely believe it. At first, he had doubted her, but the more she showed him, the more he knew it to be true. There wasn't any way she could have faked this, not down to this much detail. He peered around the computer, wondering where the wires were or how it stored this much information. It seemed incredible. It was almost as though she was from another world.

"You were presumed dead, I'm afraid, but this is a wonderful thing. To know that you survived here... Are there more of you?" she asked.

Ishibashi nodded solemnly and then holstered his pistol. He waved to the others to come out. One by one ,they appeared from the trees, wary of this stranger who was talking to Ishibashi, but they had implicit trust in his judgment. He stood and got

Miranda to repeat what she had just told him. It would take a long time for them to accept the truth, but it was necessary. Ishibashi couldn't believe all he had missed out on. A whole lifetime had passed in the world and so much had been accomplished in his absence, even though Japan had lost the war.

Chapter Seven

Other people from Miranda's ship came upon the shore and spoke with various people on the island to gather information. After the initial strangeness wore off, Ishibashi was happy to help, especially when Miranda told them of what she had discovered. With the testimony of the natives, she learned that it had indeed been a balloon-shaped bomb that approached the island and caused this devastation. Ishibashi had thought it was an attack from the enemy, when in fact it had been a relic from the war, from his own people. He felt ashamed for leaping to conclusions so abruptly and for killing men who did not deserve to die.

He and Miranda were sitting in his home. Suna had just brought them some tea and they ate some fruit.

"It is really wonderful what you have created here. You should be proud," she said.

"I am," Ishibashi replied.

"How did you manage it?"

Ishibashi smiled. "I was given an order and I followed it. I have tried to keep our traditions alive, but now I see I have held onto war too fiercely. The world has moved on. I'm not sure I did."

"It's only natural. I'm a little surprised that nobody found you sooner, but this place is far from the usual shipping lanes. It makes me wonder how many other people there are like you. It's a fascinating story to tell. Once you get back to the mainland, you're going to be in high demand. They'll probably make a dozen movies of you," she said with a laugh. Ishibashi lifted his cup to his lips with trembling hands. The thought of returning home filled him with anxiety.

"What's wrong?" she asked.

"I am not sure that the home I remember is the home waiting for me. Can you tell me what it is like?"

Miranda blew out her cheeks. "It's been a while since I've visited. I mean, it's like the rest of the world really. It's gotten bigger and brighter over the years. Buildings have gotten taller and taller. It's really something." She pulled her computer out again and turned the screen towards him, showing him images of a city that he barely recognized. There were new gleaming buildings and electric lights. Looking at the images, he was not filled with a sense of nostalgia or wistfulness; he wasn't filled with anything and this troubled him.

"I always thought I would long for home. I had given up hope of ever seeing it again some time ago. Now that you show me this, I realize that it is not my home anymore. It hasn't been for a long time."

"It might be different if you see it in person."

Ishibashi gave a slight shake of the head. "I do not think so. This world is not mine. I know Japan in here," he pointed to his head and then lowered his finger to his heart, "and here. I don't think that would change by seeing it again. I do not feel I should return anyway. I have shamed myself. I thought I was fighting for the right cause, for honour, but the world has progressed well by what you've shown me. We were on the wrong side all along. I should have seen this. We should have known."

"You can't blame yourself. You were fighting for your country. There's great pride in that and you've done so many wonderful things here. The odds on you surviving here and thriving the way you have are astronomical. I can't quite believe that you've achieved all this. It's really incredible! People are going to want to hear your story."

"Then perhaps you are the one who should tell it to them. I do not know how I could speak about it adequately. I have taken too long to realize that my home is here. This is where I belong."

"I think I understand," Miranda said. "I can't blame you for wanting your privacy. How did you do it though? How did you maintain such a strong bond with your people over all these years?"

"We kept to our traditions. We shared stories of our culture and our history; we tried to live up to the expectations of our ancestors. It has not always been easy, but we have tried to create a legacy. For a time, I wondered if we were the last outpost of Japan. I suppose now we are just a forgotten part of the world, a people who don't really belong anywhere."

"I don't think that's true. I think that perhaps you are the last outpost of a time that doesn't really exist anymore. Look, the world has made great strides forward, but it's not perfect. There are still people who struggle. There are still tensions between countries and a lot of people feel as though they have lost their own cultural identity as the world has gotten closer. There's something to be said for the fact that you have managed to hold onto yours. You should be proud. Everyone here seems happy and healthy."

"Thank you for your kind words," Ishibashi said, bowing his head. There was a pensive look on his face as he asked a question that he almost didn't dare to ask, but he knew he had to otherwise he would never have another opportunity. "This device of yours can find out anything, yes?"

"Within reason," Miranda conceded.

"Could it find out what happened to someone I knew a long time ago?"

"Possibly. We can have a look at least. Who is it that I should be looking for?"

Ishibashi gave her Keiko's name. Her fingers danced upon the keyboard and then she turned it towards Ishibashi. "Is this her?" she asked.

Ishibashi's eyes were filled with tears. His heart opened up with sorrow as he looked at the image of the woman he had once loved. In the picture, she was much older than he remembered and it was evident that she had lived far more of her life without him than with him, but he could still see the same twinkle in her eyes that he had fallen in love with all those years ago. This was the woman he had promised himself to and perhaps, although the world had moved on, it would be worth returning to see her again, even if it was just for a brief moment.

"What does it say?" he asked, his voice trembling with emotion.

"It says that... it says that she died three years ago," Miranda said, her voice catching on her words. Ishibashi was overwhelmed with an entirely new feeling of sorrow. It was one thing to know that the world wasn't the same, but quite another to learn that the woman he had loved so deeply had died.

"What?" he gasped.

"I'm sorry. It says here that she died of natural causes after a long and happy life, surrounded by her children and grandchildren. She was special to you, wasn't she?" Miranda asked.

Ishibashi nodded. "We were going to be married when I returned from the war. I wasn't supposed to be gone forever. Oh, Keiko, I'm sorry... She must have been so hurt when she thought I had died. I wonder if...I wonder if she ever thought about me."

Despite the sadness of the moment, Miranda wore a smile. "It says that her eldest son was called Ishi. She must have named him after you," Miranda smiled. "From what I'm reading here, she lived a long and full life."

"That's good. I'm glad she was happy," Ishibashi said, although deep in his heart, he lamented the fact that they hadn't been able to live that life together. Only a few people were so blessed though; at least she had not lived her life in sorrow. It made him wonder if he should have let go earlier and settled down, but there was little point in thinking about such things now.

Miranda stayed for a little while, talking with Ishibashi about various matters and telling him everything he wanted to know about the modern world.

"Are you sure you don't want to go back?" she asked.

Ishibashi nodded. "I don't believe there is anything waiting for me there. Everyone I used to know is dead. Everything I used to know has changed. There is no place for me there. My life is here now. This is where I have built my future and it's where I must stay. But I wanted to thank you for everything you have shown me. It is... remarkable what has happened over the years. I could never have imagined the world turning out like this. I am glad the war ended. I am glad that peace won."

"As am I," Miranda bowed her head. "It has been an honour to meet you. This day will live long in my memory."

"As it will in mine," Ishibashi said.

He walked with her to the beach as the others left. Supplies had been given to the people on the island and everyone had been in awe at the technology on display. There had been offers for people to return as well, but everyone on the island had built a life for themselves and nobody had a great inclination to leave. The island was their home and this is where they were going to stay. But the arrival of these outsiders had brought some closure to Ishibashi's soul. He returned to his bedroom and picked up his old army shirt that held the picture of Keiko inside. He took it to a hidden part of the woods to bury it in the soft dirt. He brought the picture to his lips and then set her to the ground, feeling as though it was only right now that her soul had been freed from its mortal prison.

He returned to Suna, whose eyes glistened with tears.

"I thought you were going to leave," she said as she flung her arms around him.

"I'm staying," he said, gently caressing her back. "My place is here with you. It always has been. I'm sorry that I haven't been able to show you that until now."

She shuddered in his arms. Ishibashi knew he would never quite understand why a woman this young and beautiful would love an old man like him, but instead of questioning it, he decided to finally accept it. This was his home and she was his family. He closed his eyes and he nodded once in affirmation of the fact that he had carried out his orders.

Captain Ryu would have been proud.

Chapter Eight

Nagasawa and Hana stood on the scorched ashes of the village that had been destroyed. New crops were already growing; thanks to the arrival of the outsiders, new ideas had flooded into the community. Nagasawa and the other young people had great plans for this new village that would be built to replace the old. This new era was being celebrated by a wedding between the happy couple.

Nagasawa was usually reserved, but on this day, he was beaming happily. The sun was high in the sky and shone its golden glory upon them all. There was much sadness considering all that had passed, but people were in good spirits and happy to look to the future. As was always the case, as long as some of them survived, then the entire community survived. They were glad to not have to worry about threat of war any longer either. No longer did they have to feel as though they were hiding under a shadow. The world was at peace and so were they.

Nagasawa stood proudly in the middle of a circle, with Hana by his side. Their wrists were bound together with twine.

Ishibashi led the ceremony. "This has been a time of great sorrow and great excitement. We have all questioned many things about ourselves over the past few weeks, but I am glad to see that we all chose to remain here. When I first arrived on this island, I did not think it was going to become my home. It was a place of refuge, but I always thought I would return to the country of my birth. But I have only just begun to realize that, over the years, I have become a part of this place and it has become a part of me. It is as much of a home as any as I have ever known and that is in large part to all of you. You are a great community of people and it has been the highest honour of my life to lead you. And now, it is my great privilege to announce to the world that my son is marrying, continuing the proud tradition of our people. Long may we live," he said and a great cheer rose up among the people of the island.

Nagasawa's smile widened even more as he turned to kiss his wife, who held him close. There was a ripple of applause and many wild howls as everyone congratulated them on their union. They danced and swayed and sang until they had time to themselves later.

"I have to admit that I was afraid you would leave with them when they gave us the opportunity. There has never been any part of the world that you are afraid to explore," Nagasawa said quietly, nuzzling into the nape of her neck.

"I was tempted for perhaps a moment, but I knew you wouldn't come with me. Where would be the fun in that?" she said, her eyes sparkling as brightly as the stars.

Nagasawa frowned. "I hope you're not implying that I prevented you from leaving."

"Of course not," Hana rocked back and forth on his lap, draping her arms around his neck. "I want to be with you. *That* is the greatest adventure. What could possibly be better than that? Besides, there is another adventure waiting for us as well. You know how your father tells you stories? Well, you are going to have to learn how to tell them now." As she said this, she placed Nagasawa's hand on her stomach and comprehension rippled across his face. They kissed deeply and, after a night of rejoicing together, Nagasawa raced away to tell his father.

Ishibashi was a wizened man and he wasn't too surprised that something like this had happened. However, he was still overjoyed for them. He congratulated his son and the two of them looked out towards the ocean, knowing they were where they belonged, knowing that that although they were far from the home of their ancestors, they were still keeping the spirit of Japan alive. The world might have changed, but on this small island at least tradition stayed strong.

Chapter Nine

Miranda was sitting alone in a wide room as the ship streaked through the water, leaving the island and its strange inhabitants behind. There was an array of maps spread out in front of her, although in truth she couldn't concentrate on work, which was incredibly unusual for her. She had been struck by how touched Ishibashi had been by the memories of the woman he had lost. Despite being on this island for so long, he had not lost the memories of his life before this; she wondered if he would have chosen to go back to Japan if this woman had still been alive. But she was also struck by the resoluteness of his spirit. He had stayed true to his honour and his duty when it must have been so easy to give up. He had kept to his orders and he had continued the fight not knowing who had won the war or even if the war was still going.

Jack and Ben came in, each of them holding a mug of coffee. Jack's arm was in a sling and they were in the middle of a conversation.

"I still think it's wrong to leave. We should be bringing them back. They killed innocent men," Jack said.

"They thought we were at war. They thought it was an invasion. In hindsight, we should have sent a messenger first or perhaps waited at night," Ben replied.

"So, you're saying that it's our fault? I didn't come here expecting to lose people. I can't believe you're happy that we just left," Jack growled, glaring at Ben.

"None of us are happy, Jack, but there's not much we can do. They didn't know any better. Can you imagine what it must have been like for them, living all these years believing that the war was still going on? They thought they might have been the last survivors," Miranda said.

"That's not an excuse," Jack said. Miranda knew she wasn't going to change his mind on this.

"At least we got what we came for. We know what has been causing these forest fires now and I'm going to devise a way that we can track them to ensure that it doesn't happen again. We'll have to get in touch with the Japanese government to see if they can tell us how many of these were actually released. I'd like to say there can't be too many of them out there after all this time, but after what we've just seen, I'm not willing to rule anything out," Miranda said.

"I can't believe all they've accomplished. I was half tempted to stay there myself," Ben said, laughing a little.

Jack grunted. "Maybe you should have. I wouldn't want to live in a back water like that. It's a dirty place and they're behind the times. What good is living there going to do? You two are acting like we came upon some lost civilisation or something. They're just people who got stranded on an island."

"You're wrong, Jack... They're more than that," Miranda said. "The way they survived is a testament to them. They could have succumbed to infighting and bickering a long time ago. But they managed to stay together as a single community. We just witnessed something truly remarkable and it makes me think about my own life. When you think about the world today, we imagine that it's been a straight line of progression, but I'm not sure we always realize everything we've lost. Since we've opened the lines of communication throughout the world, things have come together, but they have also become more fragmented as well. It's easy to lose ourselves and the traditions of the past, but traditions are what have kept these people together. They saved these people. I think we should take stock and learn from them. It's important to remember where we're coming from just as much as looking forward to where we're going."

She glanced out of the window to the island that had already receded from view and the people who would be forgotten again. They would become an amusing footnote in history, but to her, they were so much more. She made it a point to seek out her parents when she returned home and ask them about her own traditions and history. That was the legacy of these people. It wasn't that they focused on the war; it was that they could inspire others to hold onto the good parts of the world that had been left behind.

The ship sailed away from the island and back into the modern world. Miranda had come here to find the solution to a mystery, but she ended up taking much more back with her. She smiled and wondered if one day she would have a child to whom she could tell this story. It hadn't really been at the forefront of her mind so far, but after spending time with the islanders, she suddenly had an urge to put down roots and leave behind a legacy of her own.

End of an Era?

Air Force One streaked across America, a gleam in the sky to anyone who saw it pass overhead. To many, it would have been a sign of the future, but to the outgoing President of the United States, it was the end of an era, a premature one as well. The life he had planned for himself had been aborted, all because of conspiracies and lies and damned stupid people who didn't know what was good for them. He forced a smile as he walked through Air Force One, listening to the muttered shocks of his colleagues and compatriots who expressed their disbelief that it had all ended like this.

"I thought we had it in the bag."

"All the data pointed to us winning."

"We had a strategy. *A strategy!* They've royally screwed us and I don't know how they did it. How the hell did these liberals manage to convince everyone that they were right? It's a damned shame, a damned shame at all."

The voices rang out one after the other, a chorus of indignant men and women who had all devoted their lives and a considerable amount of their wealth to the glorious future of America, a future that was now in tatters. No doubt the liberals would run the country into the ground, scattering money around as though they were sowing seeds. It was poison to the America that the President had been brought up to love. It sickened him how they were twisting the American ideals to serve their own agendas.

The American Dream had become a nightmare; he couldn't help but feel responsible for it.

Perhaps if he had tried more, perhaps if he had *done* more... but no; what more could he have done? He had built himself up from nothing, clawed his way to the highest office in the land and even then there were bigger things than him, forces that he couldn't control. The damn minorities who guided the country's agenda never supported him. They tried to crush the bills he introduced and sought to disparage him in the press. All the maggots came out then, baying for blood, each one of them with an axe to grind just because they were jealous of him. It was lucky for them that the President wasn't as vindictive or petty as they were because he would have retaliated viciously. But he had to rise above it, for he was better than them.

Still, it hurt him that the people had been so stupid as to install a doddering old fool in the Oval Office. The man could barely string two sentences together without getting his words messed around. How did he pass the mental examination? He wasn't a real man either. "Just look at his wife, the shrew," he thought to himself. She wasn't young and glamorous. There were even sick and disgusting rumours that there was something going on with his granddaughter, and she wasn't even attractive! God, it wasn't as though she was as beautiful as the President's daughter.

He shook his head as anger boiled inside him. Thankfully, the crimson hue of anger didn't show through his tan.

"Don't worry, guys. You all did your best. The country doesn't know what's best for them right now. They'll be the ones paying the price in the end. At least we had a chance to do some good in this world," the President said in an effort to reassure all those who had worked tirelessly for him. At least that's what they claimed. He said the words through gritted teeth. Secretly he wondered how many of them had failed him. This loss was all on them. He should have won the election, but somewhere along the way, they must have dropped the ball. He couldn't blame the girls; they were probably too distracted by the sheer force of his masculinity and maybe intimidated too. That's probably why most of the women had voted for the other guy. He was harmless and, since he was old and frail, their motherly instincts kicked in. The President was just too potent for his own good. If only he could have sat down with each of them and told them that there was nothing to worry about. If only…if only…

A lot of the staff were still analysing what went wrong, trying to see how things could have been different. It didn't matter now. The President had actually asked NASA if time travel was possible just in case he needed to go back and fix a few things, but they had told him it wasn't. Bunch of useless people who thought they were smarter than they actually were. At least he had his loyal followers who would carry on the fight. They were the real patriots – men and women who were not afraid to wear the flag on their sleeves and march into hell, to tear the liberal masks off the faces of the monsters and show the world their true colours. It was a fight that was bigger than the President, a fight that he couldn't win even though he had given it everything.

And that was a hard thing to admit, probably the hardest thing the President ever had to do. He'd previously succeeded at everything he tried, at least when he tried it alone. Whenever other people got involved, they invariably messed it up and he wondered if he would have done better running as an independent, where he only had himself to rely on. No doubt someone would have found some way to sabotage him though. He was only one man; how was he supposed to take on the whole world when it was against him?

For some reason people were against having someone to take care of them. They spoke about liberty and freedom, but when someone came along who knew what was best for them, they rejected him and fought against him, and he didn't understand why. Was it just that they didn't believe they were worthy of being led by him? Sometimes that seemed to be the only thing that made sense.

Someone offered the President a drink and a hamburger, so he took it. The burger was just how he liked it, cooked through all the way without any of that disgusting pink stuff. It would have made a good last meal. There was nothing more American than a hamburger.

"We'll think of a way to come back from this, sir, don't you worry about that. We already have our best people on it. We'll have a plan. We're not ready to give up the fight yet. That's what this country is about. We never know when we're beaten. We didn't give up during the revolution and we're not going to give up now. God wants us to win, so we'll find a way."

The President suppressed a laugh. God was the most liberal one of all, but the President liked the zeal in this man's face. It was just a shame that the plan was doomed. Before the President had a chance to reply, a phone was thrust into his hand.

His jaw clenched when he realized it was his solicitor.

"I'm sorry to call you now, Mr. President. I know that you probably have a lot of other things on your mind, but I'm not sure this can wait. I just received word from your wife's solicitor that she is filing for divorce. Now, given everything that's going on, she has agreed to be discreet and that it need not be revealed to the press until an appropriate time, but she does want the matter officially sorted quickly."

The President barked out a laugh.

"Tell her she'll have her answer soon enough, but right now I have more important things to deal with," he said and ended the call while his solicitor was in the middle of a sentence. He shook his head. Even his own wife was betraying him, falling on her sword because she didn't feel herself worthy of standing beside him through this failure. Not that it mattered anymore. He had never really loved her anyway. She had been good for photo ops and a warm body when he needed it, but recently she had become cold and withdrawn. "Good riddance," he thought.

But still, it was another person who was leaving him and it made him wonder how blind he had truly been. How had he surrounded himself with so many weak people without realizing it until it was too late? If he had just showed better judgment, then perhaps this could all have been avoided. It was a shame that he was too trusting, too willing to give people the benefit of the doubt. They ended up taking advantage of him. Good men always became the victims of scurrilous, corrupt individuals; he was no exception.

He was about halfway up the plane now, taking in the faces of everyone who was with him. When the results had been called, their faces had been ashen, as though each of them had been convinced that victory had been absolute and inevitable. The mood on the plane had been one of celebration, but the drinks that had earlier been raised to toast success were now glugged down in remorse and mourning. It had been the President's idea to fly on Air Force One as the results were announced. Either it would be a grand return to the White House or it would be... something else. The President thanked everyone and shook their hands. They all said they would be ready to fight for the next campaign to reclaim the White House. They were loyal soldiers, terriers that were eager to return to battle despite their scars not having fully healed yet, and the President would always remember their service and their faith, and he would always be grateful for it.

But running another campaign would not be easy. Sure, his supporters were frothing at the mouth and no doubt he could inspire more jaded people to take up the cause. But the liberal media had such a stranglehold on the news that it was difficult to get the truth out; his messages would only be garbled and scrambled. They would do anything they could to discredit him and make him look like a buffoon. They already had BS lawsuits lined up to try and keep him tied up in court rather than out there with the people where he belonged. All the charges were false and he knew none of them were going to stick, at least they shouldn't, but the liberals were tricky and they had him in their targets. It wouldn't surprise him if they falsified evidence and got their cronies to lie to take him down. He had tried to protect himself by appointing loyal patriots to important offices, but he wasn't sure it was enough. The liberals hated anyone who tried to wrench power from their ugly little hands and, if he started another campaign, the President would only be slandered again. He didn't want his memory to be tainted like that.

No, he had to make a grand statement to the world, a statement that showed he was going out on his own terms because he was in control of his destiny, not the liberals. They could try to shackle him, they could try to humiliate him, but they would never succeed because he was stronger than they were. That was just something that they would never understand. They couldn't comprehend because they were so dumb and weak, their head always filled with lies from childhood. Not like the President; he had always known the truth. His father had shown it to him from a young age, rewarding him when he proved himself strong and cunning, showing nobody any mercy because they didn't deserve it. The rest of his family didn't understand, but that was because they were failures too.

Failure, failure...

For a man who had defined himself by success, the President's life had been surrounded by failure. He had always tried to be optimistic, to look for opportunities, but after being President, the world was bleak and everything else lost its allure. Where was he supposed to go from here? He was trapped by the liberal agenda and, even thought all these people were willing to follow him into Hell, he knew that it was ultimately hopeless. The world had shifted. They had chosen evil over good, wrong over right, and there could be no convincing them otherwise. The President had always known what he would do if he failed to win the election and he had always been a man to follow through on his plans.

Those in the plane didn't realise that he was giving them a final goodbye. They were all planning for the future without understanding that there could be no future. Not for them, and certainly not for him. This election had been all or nothing. The President wasn't going to watch his name and reputation be dragged through the mud through superfluous lawsuits and false allegations. He wasn't going to let himself be seen as a failure. The liberals might have won the Presidency, but they weren't going to win him.

He made his way to the front of the plane, approaching the entrance to the cockpit.

"I'm sorry, sir, but you can't go back there," a pretty stewardess said. Any other time, the President would have returned her smile and gone about his business, but not today.

"I'm still the President for a little while longer and I can go where I want," he barked. The stewardess relented and opened the door for him. He wore a smug smile, enjoying this display of power. He closed the door behind him. The cockpit was filled with blinking lights and a bright blue sky stretched out of the front window. The two pilots turned and noticed him. They were about to start and tell him to leave before they realized who he was.

"Can we help you, Mr. President?" the head pilot asked.

"Not at all, I was just making my way through the plane thanking everyone and telling them how grateful I am for their service. I know it's not protocol for me to be in here, but I wanted to personally thank you as well. You've done a really great job flying this plane for me. It's been a joy to have so many wonderful trips around the world and I'll be sure to keep your names handy when I need pilots for my private jets," he smiled. The pilots thanked him and seemed suitably honoured that he would offer them such individual praise.

"I do envy you," the President continued, leaning against the pilots' chairs. "You're lucky men to be able to see our beautiful country from this perspective." It really was a grand sight, but when the President looked down at the land below him, he was overwhelmed with a sense of disdain. Bile rose in the back of his throat for this was a land that was tainted with betrayal. It was filled with people who had turned their backs on him and believed the lies. They taunted him, mocked him, for they were consumed by their own jealousy. It would have been better to see it burn.

"It really is, sir. We're privileged people," one of the pilots said. It was the last thing he ever said. The President reached into his jacket and pulled out a gun. His fingers curled around the trigger and squeezed, for he was a man who did not flinch when something was required of him. One pilot slumped forward. The other looked around in shock, but he wasn't quick enough to react. Another shot was fired, this one striking the man square in the nose. Blood poured out. The President dragged them out of their seats. There was a hammering on the door, but he ignored it. He placed the gun down and took a seat in front of the controls. The expanse of America stretched before him. He would give them something to remember. He would make sure that his name wasn't dragged through the mud. There would be no divorce, no lawsuits. Hell, technically he hadn't even relinquished the Presidency because he would die before the other guy got sworn in.

That's what he had wanted more than anything – to be President for life – and now his dreams were coming true.

The plane teetered and veered as he took the controls and made the nose dive. The plane whined and behind him he heard the panicked screams of all the passengers, but he didn't care about them. They had devoted their lives to him. This is exactly what they had signed up for. A serpent smile widened across the President's face and a glaze came over his eyes as he saw the noble land of his birth get closer and closer, rushing towards him at breakneck speeds. The plane shook and shuddered, but his hands never left the controls. He was a man of conviction, a man who knew when to go out on top. He was a man in control of his own destiny.

When there was no chance for the plane to escape its fate, he rose and flung open the door. The passengers were shocked, climbing over each other to try and make sense of this. They looked up at him, rapt in awe as they always were. He spread out his arms as if to embrace them.

"I made it, Ma! I'm top of the world!"

Many Thanks to:-

Christa Gecheva: cover images

Robert Spake: Editing and Input.

Gabriela Lakatos: Proofreading and copy editing.

Scott Gaunt: cover graphics

Printed in Great Britain
by Amazon